PRAISE FOR *THE LIVING DAYS*

"Beautifully written, visceral, and ecstatic. Unafraid, as angels might be, to bear witness to the force of entropy pulling us all toward death."

—**PRETI TANEJA, author of** *We That Are Young*

"Jeffrey Zuckerman's translation is perfect in its power and precision. A magnificent gem."

—**JENNIFER CROFT, translator of** *Flights*

"The finest Mauritian novelist at work today, Ananda Devi has long been the francophone voice of the outcast, the oppressed, and the derelict. This fluid translation of one of her darkest works gives the reader a glimpse at her profound talent and her unique ability to synthesize political rage with poetic lyricism."

—**ADAM HOCKER, Albertine**

THE LIVING DAYS

ANANDA DEVI

Translated by Jeffrey Zuckerman

FEMINIST PRESS
AT THE CITY UNIVERSITY
OF NEW YORK
NEW YORK CITY

Published in 2019 by the Feminist Press
at the City University of New York
The Graduate Center
365 Fifth Avenue, Suite 5406
New York, NY 10016

feministpress.org

First Feminist Press edition 2019   DEC 1 3 2019

 This book is supported in part by an award from the National
ART WORKS. Endowment for the Arts.
arts.gov

 This book was made possible thanks to a grant
from New York State Council on the Arts with the
support of Governor Andrew M. Cuomo and the
New York State Legislature.

This book is supported in part by the Institut français, Paris.

First printing November 2019

Edited by Cécile Menon and Angeline Rothermundt (Les Fugitives)
Cover design by Sukruti Anah Staneley
Text design by Drew Stevens

Library of Congress Cataloging-in-Publication Data
Names: Devi, Ananda, author. | Zuckerman, Jeffrey, 1987- translator.
Title: The living days / Ananda Devi ; translated by Jeffrey Zuckerman.
Other titles: Jours vivant. English
Description: First Feminist Press edition. | New York, NY : Feminist Press,
    2019. | English translation of a French novel.
Identifiers: LCCN 2019015923 (print) | LCCN 2019019394 (ebook) | ISBN
    9781936932719 (E-book) | ISBN 9781936932702 (pbk.)
Classification: LCC PQ3989.2.N547 (ebook) | LCC PQ3989.2.N547 J6813 2019
    (print) | DDC 843/.92--dc23
LC record available at https://lccn.loc.gov/2019015923

THE LIVING DAYS

Unreal City,
Under the brown fog of a winter dawn,
A crowd flowed over London Bridge, so many,
I had not thought death had undone so many.
. . . .
"That corpse you planted last year in your garden,
"Has it begun to sprout? Will it bloom this year?"

—T. S. ELIOT, *The Waste Land: The Burial of the Dead*

London, 2005

Three narrow stories, three uneven hallways each three paces long: nothing more than a mousehole, a gingerbread house from which she would never escape again, inside which she could not breathe for much longer. Even so, she would go on watching, patient as an ailing she-wolf.

She only had to glance out the window to see how she might slip and fall. The gleaming surfaces, the mirror-smooth roads, the featureless faces could all pull her far away from herself, so far she would have no way of returning. There were so many ways to get lost.

The day was slick over Portobello Road.

She sat in this armchair so faded she no longer remembered what color it once was, even though she clearly recalled the day she bought it, as lighthearted, as energetic as if she had been spreading her wings for the first time. Maybe this armchair had only ever had the colors bestowed on it by her gaze that day?

With lowered eyes she considered her hands. Or rather, the paths traced on her hands, fierce furrows that left no space untouched: the surface of an unknown planet, her hands. And the strangeness of their posture at rest. Her palm formed a hollow, like a bowl, her fingers curled inward, but not gracefully: sharply, contorted by thick bones, with a far darker color than the rest of her wholly pale skin.

These hands had become talons, but talons incapable of grabbing or crushing any prey. Not that she would have wanted to crush anything. Caress, yes; stroke, yes; trace curves, yes: gentleness, after all, was what she had once represented in her distant youth.

Gentleness had shaped Mary; sweet, sweet Mary Rose as her parents had called her, and her sisters had mimicked them mockingly as if they wanted to blot out their timid, delicate sister. Who, as a small child, had been like a porcelain doll, then, as she grew up, more like a stork, slender, slightly hunched over, eternally indecisive, smiling that smile that conveyed to everyone around her the terror flitting just beneath her surface.

Her smile, her soft lower lip, her eyes so pale that they nearly disappeared, the precocious groove between her brows, had ensnared her as she grew up. She had been reduced to a talcum-and-lavender Mary, her hands always at work on bows for presents, bouquets of flowers, small decorative trinkets, lacework and knitting and crochet, all that, yes, a very good girl, upright and sensible, but not a girl to ride or screw or fuck, as we might so crudely put it these days, but why not, those words say exactly what they mean, why bother with coy euphemisms, really, what's the point?

She was fifteen during the war. Fifteen was the age when girls had to take whatever they could get, kissing all those dashing boys in their tight army uniforms, luring them with their bodies, their hair, their embraces, their desires, why pretend when time is so short, why act as if this whole little game wouldn't end this way, with sex in all its forms, indoors, in cars, in the countryside, in fields of wheat, among trees, clouds, storms, as bombs fell, sex ripping apart cheap clothes and ruining set hair and straining sweet skin? How good it must have felt to claim some right to them, to have some hold on those handsome, sturdy, rugged men from the countryside, to relish that energy all too quickly gone as their trains bore them away to their inescapable fates! And parents pretended not to see anything because that was what being patriotic meant at that time, putting your tongue in a boy's mouth, putting your hand on his crotch to tell him to come back, telling him to fight but also to take care of himself, telling him not to lose hope at the worst, when fear broke out and flesh split apart and bones jutted out of wounds and faces were half gone, promise me you'll come back, all right I will, and the memory of a kiss, the red trace of a kiss, the swelling of a kiss would not disappear, not even when their eyes were opened to the pointlessness of war at the exact moment so many other eyes were closed for having seen it up close.

But not Mary. At fifteen she was a good girl, so timid that the word itself seemed to have been invented for her, a wallflower, truly, the soft, pale, fragrant flower that sank into the wallpaper during parties while other mouths greedily lunged forward to claim what had been promised them. Wallflower—what a nice, insipid, even stupid word, there weren't any flowers on the walls, they were only on her dress, flowers aplenty, that horrible muslin dress chosen by her father for her fifteenth birthday, with such delight in his eyes as he offered it to her that she could not possibly dream of saying "I don't want it," the joy in his eyes was that of giving a gift, and the dress, even if it was ugly, gathered in all the wrong spots to emphasize her lack of breasts, not a tight skirt that would hug her hips, no, a hideous floating, flowery, gathered dress was what she had to wear, and it doomed her to becoming the wallpaper flower that nobody invited to dance despite her sandy blue eyes, despite her charming lips, despite her smile which promised the brightest of gifts: she sighed and sipped the punch that went to her head and she watched the other girls dancing and she sighed again.

But, by some miracle, that evening, the last one before the big day, that wasn't how it ended, was it, Mary Grimes? Oh, you're looking away, you're hiding those hands that are nothing like the ones you had at fifteen, those weren't talons, no, not those hands with soft palms, pink nails, hands ready to be grabbed, tapping a rhythm you liked so much on your knees, why would you look away from the memory of your greatest glory?

Fifteen years old during the war, one last party before the men sail off, and you, too, preparing to go, to abandon that house with green shutters you and your family live in, that claustrophobia of dead souls, that illusion of warmth which turns to ice as soon as the door opens onto other silences. Only when he's drowned in booze would your father offer you this dress, otherwise he'd never think to do it. Only in those rare moments when the day's heat has finally escaped the rafters would your mother stop fixating on her swollen ankles, and only then does she remember sweet, sweet Mary. You know this is how it's always been in the English countryside, and especially in the village of Benton-on-Bent, on the river Bent, a name that had not yet acquired the sexual connotations it would hold much later and which for you merely evoked bends carved deep by habit.

And so, that night, she wore her wallflower dress, knowing as soon as she put it on that this would be her sole role, and she set aside her dreams as she walked out with a maturity at odds with her youth. Not tonight, she told herself with a weary smile, tonight won't be the night.

But that was not how it came to be. Amid the gentle swaying of bodies, as a prelude to coupling, someone noticed Mary Grimes, sitting down, tapping her feet, that orange punch slowly getting her drunk. He walked up to her. In the semiobscurity, and because he stood in front of the light in the village hall, she hadn't been able to see his face. Just a vague outline of youth, of virility, a hand with bits of black under the nails offered to her and into which she put her own, thinking all the while that, for just a bit, they would float up to the ceiling. He had taken her outside, beneath a moonless sky, because it was the last night for lovers and it was the least the night could do to be wholly black. He took her far off, under the trees, and she, trembling but sure of herself, certain that it was the last chance for both of them, realizing with this lucidity so at odds with the moniker of *sweet* that had always been bestowed upon her, that he had seen everyone pairing off and had abruptly realized that he had spent too much time drinking and not enough summoning up courage and that soon there would be no girl left for his last living night, whereupon he noticed her muslin dress with pink flowers and maybe that was a sight that had delighted him, this flowery field waiting, maybe he had shrugged at this consolation prize, but all the same he had made his way toward her and she was now following him under the trees, far off under the trees with no worry other than how to do it.

In a nook even darker still, he stopped and did all the things she had lived out only in her dreams. This astonished her. She wondered how he had known, before she realized that it was a dream that everyone shared, the dreams of the body and not of the imagination, and it was the body that drove the young man to press Mary against the tree trunk and to lift up her chin, to bring his lips to hers, to open her lips with his tongue, with a little force, to explore this innocent mouth until her tongue began to tryst with his. These were the dreams of bodies that made these meetings between two people who had never seen one other before (she still hadn't seen his face) so easy, and of bodies that, standing at first, their clothes still in place, then lying on the ground, their clothes elsewhere, pressed together against one another with so much tamed fury.

For most of that time she kept her eyes shut.

Afterward, they were both delighted and disappointed. Their emotions gave way to reason once more, which confronted them with just how long their bodies had been anticipating these actions and just how swift the act itself had turned out to be. But they clung to each other with the determined tenderness of youth still under the illusion that it was wonderful, and they kissed for a long while.

After kissing, they talked, or rather he talked, and she loved his voice as she listened, with her eyes shut, while he talked about his life thus far and what he would do after, she heard about his childhood on a distant farm and the pimply years until his apprenticeship with the only mechanic in the neighboring county, who could fix bikes and farmers' tractors, she heard about his yesterdays, his tomorrows, but as for his tomorrows she knew he was making them up so he wouldn't have to consider the possibility that they might not exist, he talked of a small cottage, cotton curtains, a bit like your dress, actually (the cloth made for a bright spot on the grass nearby), some kids, he said, who'll wake us up when we just want to sleep. She wondered whether this "we" had any particular meaning, where he was going with this dream, was he just saying anything to keep from crying about the prospect of the truck he'd be loaded onto the next morning with all the others, was he talking about a future he could see, one that he was wishing for, or was he just playing a game, was he being silly, she couldn't be sure. And he kept going, he would have his own mechanic's shop in front of the house, he'd have new tools, new machines that the mechanic he'd worked for didn't even know about, soon everyone would be coming to him because he knew not only how to fix bikes and tractors but also cars, which plenty of people were starting to buy, cars, those wouldn't be like they were now, only rich people had them, no, even we'll have a car and it'll be the end of the old mechanic, a surly, ill-humored man who always gave him the filthiest jobs, a cottage, curtains, a shop, kids, a wife of course who he'd want to sleep with—and die of old age beside, but that he didn't say out loud—you know how to bake tarts, Mary, I love mirabelle tarts, I'm mad about them, I could eat them every day, and she promised to learn how to make tarts, especially with mirabelles, if he ever came back, and she wanted to ask him, when will you come back, and she worried that he might reply, never.

They parted ways before dawn, and it was only once

she had come back home, propelled toward her bedroom by a joy so unexpected that she hadn't even felt herself falling, that she realized she hadn't seen his face at all. She knew his first name, Howard, but not his last. When she thought of the cottage and the shop and the children, she didn't even know what name she might use to give some substance to her fantasies. She tried a few: Smith, Black, Rogers, Ecclestone, Preston, Baulkstead, but none of them charmed her. She would have to be satisfied with his first name. She would call herself Mary Howard (and him Howard Howard). It was a name that smiled.

She slept. In the morning she woke up knowing she would always remain Mary Grimes.

Many young men never came back. Many young women became single mothers. Not Mary, but she never saw Howard again alive. Was he dead or did he decide not to come back to see her? She preferred the first explanation. Mary, at fifteen, had become a war widow.

Her bedroom is on the third floor. A burgeoning mass of mold that eats up sleepless hours with silent chatter stipples the wallpaper. She wonders what that unmoving, open-mouthed profusion might say. What complaints, what rebellions, what papery wounds might perhaps be expressed.

On the second floor is the bathroom, with a window that never shuts, half-clogged pipes, streaks of rust on the purple linoleum. In the bathtub, now more gray than white, the water has left traces like scratches.

The living room–dining room on the ground floor has become a place not to live in but to dump the past in.

Nothing has changed in this house for ages. It's not worth the effort, any effort, to keep it tidy when one is so old and the next minute could be the last. Mary says this as a straightforward observation, without bitterness, why tempt fate, that's the dying person's superstition. And for this reason everything stays where it is, the curtains pockmarked by mites, the carpet reeking of urine—although it's not actually urine, she hasn't let herself go that far yet—the mattress on box springs sunken so deep that she has to sleep on the edge, and even the hole in the ceiling over the bed, once small but now grown to the size of a two-pound coin. A small hole that opens in the middle of the night on a great unknown. She'd rather not think about it.

She's now at the point of no longer caring. So used to things decaying that it's ceased to bother her; on the contrary, they're her own ruins. Ruins reminiscent of those of London on that spring day when, at just twenty-five, she became for the first time conscious of its corpses and promises, ruins that she gladly contemplates at a remove because nothing outside the window looks like her anymore: she's a stranger in a strange century.

A city of corpses and promises, yes.

Ten years after the war, and Benton-on-Bent is adorned with a huge shell hole, just one, on the outskirts of the miraculously spared town. The village council debates whether to fill it in or to keep it as a memento of that terror; but there are far more important holes to fill.

Mary was always doomed to her role as a good girl—soon an old girl—who took care of her parents as her father's face became ruddier and ruddier while her mother's enormous legs became harder and harder for her to walk with. Beached seals, she thought, stuck on a gray shore where they'd flop around until they asphyxiated. Elsewhere, the war had changed everything. Elsewhere, they were starting to rebuild, but here in the countryside, everyone went on as they always had. The countryside was now bereft of its young, healthy men. As she made her way down to the village, she unconsciously kept track of how many young men she walked past, just the same way she'd played that game of counting all the bikes on the road between the plum trees and the apple trees when she was younger. But now it wasn't a game. She walked by teenagers, yes, but they were wan and hunched by their secret shame of not being old enough to go and get killed. And old men, too, old men everywhere, frozen and twisted, hungrily gulping down the fresh, green air those boys could no longer enjoy.

The air that Howard should have been breathing. The air that should have bathed Howard the day he was supposed to come back from France victorious, wounded, matured, ennobled, handsome, and rather than go to his house he should have come straight here, to her house, since she had given him her address before leaving (but why then had he never written to her?), and he would have knocked on her door, and the first thing she would have seen upon opening the door would have been this luminous air redolent of herbs and spices, this air of thyme and rosemary, as in that syncopated ballad two American boys would sing thirty years later, *parsley, sage, rosemary and thyme*—and without a word they would have kissed, she would have taken care not to clasp him too tightly because of the wound on his right side, and, just like this first time, he would have done everything exactly as she had dreamed he might.

The only problem with Mary's dreams was that she couldn't put a specific face to Howard. She saw a uniform, a man a full head taller than her, a mass of black hair (but could she be sure it had been black? That night, the gleaming light seemed, the more she thought about it, to have had a reddish tinge), she saw fleeting, changing features that sometimes outlined the face of Errol Flynn as Robin Hood, stealing her heart, and sometimes to her astonishment that of Johnny Weissmuller, the swimmer who had played Tarzan. This ever-shifting face prevented her from refining and fine-tuning her dreams. The shadows hiding him had been a gloomy omen, deepening the physical distance between them, bluntly reminding her that it had only been one night, just one, not even that, half a night, a fragment of a night, and that she had never seen his face.

After some months, when she started to forget the things he had told her during their only conversation, she set them down in a diary. She knew it would prove to be the most important event of her life. But the years went by and all that remained of that memory were these words, which, in this way, themselves became the memory—fleshless, insubstantial shapes. Howard, the real one, with those grease-stained fingers, his straightforward ambitions, the smile in his voice as he talked about cars, the fear in his voice when he contemplated an uncertain future, came to be replaced by Howard Howard, half Flynn, half Tarzan, swinging on a vine of passion to pull Mary from her town, from her family, from her countryside, and most of all from her Grimes.

As she waited, she forced down spoonfuls of her mother's plum custard on Sundays, she dreamed of those mirabelle tarts she had never learned to make, while lumpy custard stuck to the insides of her mouth, leaving behind a cold film, a trace of frustration; no, more than frustration, a blockage so complete that she almost felt like her own body was trying to expel some decomposing matter from her mouth, and something in her was boiling, foaming, threatening to break out even as on the outside she remained calm and impassive and she kept on eating her pudding to the rhythm of her father's noisy swallowing.

But maybe there was a god watching over Mary. A few

years after the end of the war, her grandfather died, leaving her his small house in London on Portobello Road, famed for its antiques, its glorified flea market, thereby granting her an escape from Benton-on-Bent and its custard. Sweet Mary, rosy Mary, Mary the rose, *rosemary and thyme*, decided to go to London and see if she could find some trace of Howard. And even if she didn't find him, she'd still have managed to escape her mother's plum custard, her father's smacking lips and the terrible monotony of those winter days.

A house wedged into a row of ten completely identical homes bearing the charming name of a terraced house that itself was utterly uncharming, houses crammed together, each one equally dark and lackluster, cold, with dilapidated paneling, a skimpy cardboard house of three stories that would be hers for the rest of her life and that she would come to love with the long, unwavering devotion of those born with nothing to live for.

This house, already decrepit by the time she came to live there, came to be her passport to London when she had already thrown her hopes into the overflowing emptiness of her parent's rubbish bins.

The day she arrived in London, she walked slowly down Portobello Road, echoing the rhythm of the street itself, borne by the springtime smiles as sunshine flowed into every corner of her body. She stumbled at moments, dazed by so much light as the world came out of its darkness and began to vibrate like the start of a jazz tune in her thoughts and like the swish of heavy skirts that almost felt extravagant after the wartime shortages.

The first thing she had done was to buy a beret on Portobello Road, just because the woman selling it had called her *my dear*, not with the frown of pity people usually gave her but with genuine tenderness. They had looked each other right in the eyes and smiled as if they were both welcoming, in conspiracy, this new world. The woman had handed the beret to Mary as if it were already hers. That one and no other. Mary had never worn anything like it in her life. Back in the countryside, people did dust off their hats for special occasions, with flowers or fruits or birds placed on top, but this beret, which she took with a trembling hand and set on her head, transformed her completely. The woman leaned out of her stall and, with a steady hand, adjusted the angle. In the mirror, a young woman with a coquettish smile faced Mary. She paid, giving no thought to the cost, and started walking again, noticing how the beret changed the way she walked, the way she held her head, the idea she had of herself: she was no longer a terrified little mouse.

What she now saw in London was an energy born out of so much death, a refusal to fold, a refusal to concede the scope of the massacre, a collective, steely, fiery determination to forget the air-raid sirens, the roars of the bomber planes, the whistling of artillery shells, to forget the rationing, to forget the young men who had sailed off and the old men now orphaned. A desire for a rebirth so complete that it would turn once and for all the page on which the end of days had been inscribed in red ink, so complete that it would result in a flood of new children to supplant all the fighters who had been lost, children who would bear the stigmata of the war and who would refuse to rush back into its logic and its blindness, children of peace, yes, these were the illusions that arose from the ruins of the city, everywhere, everywhere a rosy air like what remained of Regent's Park in this springtime of its new life, an air perfumed with *rosemary and thyme*, this city is for you, Mary, it baptizes you with a red beret as a way of bidding farewell to the countryside.

The children were already running after each other through the rubble. The youngsters were already embracing the city. And the old people came there both to sigh and to remind themselves that the war was over, that they could look up and see not the bulging shadows of the plane bays releasing bombs but a sky scrubbed of all threats. They were fortunate not to know how impermanent that peace would be. The children believed in their good luck, because they had survived. In their memories they could still hear the farewell songs of the dead soldiers, as well as the reedy, triumphant chant of the lucky ones. Secretly, they were happy, they started to believe that they had survived, that they were still here, that they could pick up the bricks at their feet and rebuild the world. Soon, Peggy Lee would sing *you give me fever*, and that fever would seize them at the dances, in the ballrooms, in the bedrooms, with a seductive snap of the fingers.

Oh, this spring day, Mary Grimes refused to believe in those terrible stories people told about the capital. The industrial era had entered a glorious phase in which it was still drowning the city in its pea-soup fog but also heralding a once-forgotten prosperity. How could she not believe, not throw herself body and soul into all these hopes and dreams, not sing and dance in the wake of this monster's downfall and in the knowledge that she had been on the winning side? They had every right to be proud. The future lay at her feet, hidden beneath her red beret; she took a brazen step forward and tried to avoid the ruts, she didn't know that it rained here as if the city was trying to flush all its sins out of the ground and that the chill, when it seeped into the city, would be nothing like the chill of the countryside that reddened cheeks and burned the lungs, as the old folks like to say; rather, it made everyone so sad they could just melt. She was young, she had been caught by London fever, she kept the memory of a man between her legs, she too was rising out of these ashes, and, as she held out her hand and received a raindrop as thick as a tuberculosis patient's phlegm, she saw a good omen but nothing more.

She had seen the house inherited from her grandfather and had immediately decided to leave her parents' village forever, that English countryside more moribund than the cratered and ravaged city, the city ruined in a different way, ruined by people suddenly become outmoded, escapees from the war who still hadn't realized that the world now did things differently, that nothing was as it had once been, that the downward spiral had been overcome, that the changes of this second half of the century would petrify the earth and terrify nature, that tomorrow this little country would no longer be the master of the universe but would return to its normal dimensions, its isolation making it even smaller and reinforcing its boundaries.

Of course, none of this was known to Mary, but she, in her rustic simplicity, was convinced by the red beret or by the sun on Portobello Road, or by those craters that hadn't kept life from going on here, to move in and spread her wings. In all the shop windows along the street she saw the proof of a kind of crazy vitality. Here, people survived by selling antiques or simulacra of antiques or motley objects or anything at all, and in this way they had all, she presumed, overcome the madness of this war, and certainly here, only here, on this street strangely detached from time, death had carved out some space for the seeds of the future.

She, too, had been energized by this new faith and now decided to make objects. Like all these people—men and women, young and old, maimed and whole—unsure of what to do with their hands, she registered for arts and crafts courses. Every student there was different but their eyes all shared the same golden gleam. In shaping plaster and clay, she had discovered a joy so unexpected, so distinct from her being that she could almost believe that she was still asleep in her natal landscape and that the strange shapes being made by her fingers had come from the pink of her dreams.

Statuettes, egg cups, bowls, teacups and candlesticks: these made up the collection of objects that were not just the charming evidence of her earliest attempts and her lack of talent but were in fact so visibly handcrafted that they caught the eye of enough buyers to enable her to survive. In this way, she learned that on Portobello Road everything could be sold, as long as it had heart in it.

That people bought things she had made never stopped surprising her. The connoisseurs who often stopped by the market invariably glanced quickly at the stall in front of the house with the blue door and immediately kept on walking. But the passersby and idlers always lingered, as if attracted despite themselves, despite the lumps and bumps, or perhaps because of those, because these rough-hewn things touched them, because they suggested survival and defiance.

Mary took her inspiration from Portobello Road itself

and reproduced her street in miniature, the lady selling knickknacks who brewed beer in her cellar by fermenting strange concoctions that reeked so strongly of yeast and sugar that it drove her neighbors insane; the old beggar man who sold his family's antiques but more often simply gave them to passersby because he had no idea how to hawk his wares; the young man who everybody on the street suspected of being a fence but who they all refused to report to the police; the war veteran who sold collectible objects: postage stamps, metal cigarette cases adorned with voluptuous, scantily clad women, dainty sewing kits, key rings, replicas of flags, butterflies, insects, dried flowers, stones, nails, bones, his shop with a narrow front window extending in a labyrinth that rose and fell and forked, and as visitors went from one collection to the next they realized just how a passion could turn into an obsession. Books, drawings, engravings, caricatures: everything could be found on Portobello Road. All it took was a stroll down the road to discover the world. And, over the years, this world was summed up, reproduced in miniature, in Mary's window. The shopkeepers and the craftsmen, the cleaners and the owners, the veterans and the chimney sweeps, the women with red berets and with wild scarves, the faceless soldiers of a single night and the face-painted prostitutes of another night: Mary recreated them all. She managed, with a few often-awkward shapes, to capture a posture, a sadness, a cadence; expressions that often made onlookers smile because they were reminiscent of nothing so much as the caricatures of Honoré Daumier.

In the alleys branching off the main road, the aftereffects of the war were still visible: a Salvation Army soup kitchen where survivors went to eat without having to look anyone in the eye; a homeless shelter where men creeped like fleeting shadows, the former soldiers recognizing one another by the ugly yet sturdy coats that they had been given in the army—even in spring they wore them to cover their threadbare clothes or their missing arms; veterans turned drunkards sleeping in corners; others slightly less destitute poking their heads out of their rented basement rooms like moles peeking at the sun for the first time.

When Mary walked around her London neighborhood, the mere sight of one of those coats or those limping gaits or those broad shoulders would make her jump. She watched each one carefully, hoping against hope that one of these silhouettes might prove to be Howard's. Luck alone would be what reunited them. She had kept on believing in that small possibility and gone on, at the risk of seeming impudent or indecent, scrutinizing every face in which she was sure she had caught some feature that the blight of war had carved deeply or some thousand-yard stare that the sight of bombs had set permanently. Of course, she did not know what Howard's face looked like. Maybe she hoped he would be the one to recognize her. She imagined herself meeting the gaze of one of those men and seeing that slow glimmer of recognition. A wary smile—Mary . . . Mary?—and her body would start to tremble.

Filled with these sensations, she took her shaky hands and used them to shape loving figurines, sometimes daring to create, in the thick clay, bodies that were coupled, interlocked, melding into one another, with small members thrust into open vaginas, dueling tongues, jutting nipples; but before the statues hardened she mushed them between her hands, her face red, her breath short, and she kneaded them furiously as if, while erasing them, she could imprint them in her palm and, once night had fallen, read there the erotic lines of her dreams.

In these times of starting afresh, she watched men and women playing out a dance of seduction beneath the just-flowering almond trees. Men and women saw each other, slowed down, turned to face each other and make sure that their eyes hadn't deceived them and their hearts hadn't fooled them. Was it the color of the leaves or the particular quality of the light that gave them this indecent beauty? Or was it the certainty that they had been saved from disaster and had thus been the beneficiaries of good fortune? They shifted trajectories, retraced their steps, approached one another; their gazes slid across each other's bodies. Then, quite naturally, they started walking again, this time side by side, a little smile on their lips. At the end of the street, almost without thinking about it, their hands reached out at the same time and their fingertips brushed lightly, fleetingly. At the end of the street, a life had taken root. *You give me fever* . . . Mary watched them and held back her sighs.

These newly formed couples contemplated Mary's figurines and recognized the precise gleam of the white paint on their eyes and the hint of movement in their hands about to touch. They bought these figurines, because they knew that they had been made just for them.

Love charms, death charms: these were what Mary was making, although she didn't realize it, since she thought only of Howard, nor did she realize that the pornographic figurines that had only lived momentarily in her hands, just enough time for her forehead to redden, would survive for far longer in the more dignified figurines formed from the same clay that refused to forget its original shape. They stole the breath of those who held them in their hands and plunged them into a state of trembling desire that they couldn't understand. Some lonely buyers would go to sleep with a statuette beneath their pillow, feeling shame at this childish act, and would wake up with Mary's tears on their cheeks.

Sometimes, just to rid herself of this memory that weighed her down as heavily as if she had been one of the single mothers of her village, she tried to imagine Howard's death, tried to convince herself that it had come to pass, that there had been no alternative, the only man who had ever touched her, who had taken her virginity amid a loamy, peaty fragrance that could just as easily have been hers as it could have been from the damp grass she had lain upon, this man no doubt had died at Dunkirk, sliced in half by a shell just when he was supposed to be evacuated, and he hadn't even had the time to send a thought that would be caught by the stars and read by those who loved him, his parents or a woman whose name he didn't know—his death had been instantaneous, there had been no time for farewell notes or regrets. Or maybe while he'd been sunk to his calves in the mud of the trenches his leg had been wounded by a shell explosion as he kept on shooting at the enemy, and he hadn't thought to examine it until the pain had finally snaked its way to his brain: what he finally did see was an unrecognizable mess of flesh and bone. He had been amputated: the idea of death had occurred to him. He stayed in hospital for weeks, aimless and wan. How could he come back home a cripple? He would be welcomed as a hero, of course, an object of admiration and flattery, but time would go by and interest would fade, patience would wear thin, disdain would be visible on everyone's face, and he would become what he now was: an invalid unable to be the mechanic he'd dreamed of being, unable to drive a car, unable above all to be a man. His lips pale with exhaustion, he would eventually decide that the kindest way out of his situation was simply death.

Whether he had died quickly or slowly made no difference to Mary. She still woke up alone.

Time went by, and her hopes of Howard's return faded. Her statuettes now only described absence. Yet they allowed her to feel alive, to continue her strange exploration of the world, to imagine that she was involved in things, not some insubstantial being that mirrors and glass panes just happened to reflect back.

Time went by, so fast—so slow. One day, many years later, her potter's hands stopped their work on a bit of clay they had been shaping and refused to let go.

With barely a glance, the doctor pronounced his diagnosis of rheumatoid arthritis. Eventually, he said, you won't be able to work with your hands at all. He didn't need to add that this was the first step of her descent into poverty.

She considered her hands, the purplish-blue lines of her veins where she could almost see the blood flowing, the thickness of her sharply bent fingers, and she felt betrayed by her body. She had never imagined old age coming like this, like a death sentence, rather than a slow metamorphosis; a cleaver that had come down and cut off her hands.

The clay and the plaster and the resin would stay in their airtight bags, merely hinting at what they could have become: from now on she would only be shaping them in her mind.

Overnight, the streets turned icy. The familiar paths changed direction. None of the territories that she had conquered remained hers. The damp all around her awoke pains so deep that they seemed to be embedded in her skin. She had to shut all the doors, seal the cracks and gaps, and hide under her duvet, the extra heater turned all the way up and the oil radiators expelling smoke without actually offsetting the November chill. No matter what she did, she was frozen.

Mary could no longer bear winter, but she couldn't leave. She had been reborn in this town, on this street, the very day she had come here. There was nowhere else she could possibly go. All she had was this refuge on Portobello Road.

Everything closed in around her. No matter where she went, the air was saturated and licked her with an icy tongue, constricting her, reducing her so completely that she could no longer see herself when she looked at her body: no head, no feet, no belly; just a shadow, sometimes reflected in a window pane, one of those old women people avoided seeing at all.

Until, more than sixty years after Howard, someone else came into her life to fill the void her pain had created.

Did she still have a face or had the city forced her to rub it away with her mottled fingers?

So many years had gone by. The world was no longer the same. She was so old that she was starting to disappear along with the past. A dissolution that, all too soon, would be complete.

She was no longer assured of making ends meet: her hands had betrayed her. Her old-age pension was barely enough to cover her expenses and her food. This became such an urgent concern that, one day, at the local supermarket, fixated on the cost of various tins, she had picked up dog food. The salesgirl had paused, and then, with false cheeriness, asked: Oh, so you have a dog now, dear? Mary had jumped and reddened as she realized her mistake, then, mortified, knowing that everyone could see what had happened, simply answered with a yes. She had left with five tins of Friskies. She set them on the kitchen table and stared at them. She had read the labels, which hadn't been of any help. She had turned the tins over and over in her hands.

She put on some water to heat up and carefully peeled off the labels.

That evening, through the window, London had sniggered while watching her. The sky's downward gaze had given her dinner a strange, morbid taste. This was no longer the city of her earliest days, her own city, tamed by long walks, formed by well-trodden paths rather than particular destinations. This was no longer a city of legacies and ghosts of the war. It was a city that trod old people underfoot, a crowded yet glorious city that crushed the weak and rewarded the strong. She hadn't recognized it in decades.

That night, she ate, hunched over her plate as if to hide herself, turning her face away from the weak light. Even the photographs of her dead parents seemed too heavy for her to bear. She chewed this tasteless stuff that seemed to resemble herself in its lack of flavor, a shapeless mixture of memories of what had once been alive but hadn't been for a long time, of what had lost all identity; she swallowed it all and remembered that this food was supposed to appeal to dogs, to their voracious appetites, to their fondness for raw meat. As it went into her mouth, this dog food tainted her a bloody purple, draining her of her own color. She refused to vomit, but she couldn't bring herself to look in the mirror as she brushed her teeth.

Everywhere she turned, the city was wearing the same mocking look. The parks that usually enveloped her in their turbulent greenery now evinced palpable hostility toward her. She would enter a park and immediately get hit by a Frisbee or step into dog shit or be caught in rain when, just five minutes earlier, it had been so nice out. One day, in Kew Gardens, an old horse chestnut tree that she had always loved had rained conkers upon her. She was so dumbfounded that she hadn't been able to move and a girl had to grab her hand. Are you all right, love? she'd asked with a strong cockney accent that, for once, Mary hadn't found disagreeable. But all right? No, she wasn't all right; she would never be all right again. Old age had caught her by surprise and there was no way for her to shrug it off; she was sentenced to wander through this city full of pitfalls for the elderly.

Every time the social workers came to see her, she pretended to be out. She worried that one day they might come with backup, surrounding the house and capturing her like a bird in a net. They were dying to put her in an old people's home and seize her house, this tiny house even older than Mary herself, but which would fetch a tidy profit in this neighborhood where everything had become prohibitively expensive.

It was only a matter of time. But she had promised herself that she wouldn't go without a fight.

And just as she was at her wits' end, as she struggled not to sink into invisibility, there came Cub . . .

His dreadlocks. His overlarge shirts, his army trousers, his basketball shoes. His heavy eyes, his lips. Cub.

From across the street the boy watched her, not brazenly, but calmly, self-assuredly, as if the world belonged to him—which maybe it did. To him and not to her, that old, moribund woman as pale and yellow as an autumn day in the suburb he'd come from. He seemed so firmly rooted to the ground. Nothing would dislodge him, not thunderstorms, not terror, not a hostile gaze.

From across the street, leaning against a wall, he watched her house, its crannies, the bathroom window that never shut. Mary came out of her house, she opened the front door slightly, poking her nose and her toes out as if she were wading into a chilly ocean. She undid and redid the wool scarf around her neck five times, pulled down her hat so it would cover her ears. Even so, her entire body violently protested these first steps out of her house, her feet testing the ground and finding it slippery, her mouth refusing to open and let out a sigh that would condense in the cold, her eyes already tearing up, and her hands, her hands above all, clenched tight deep within her pockets as if ready to tear into their fury and their pain.

She saw him and stopped. He went on chewing his gum, his hands stuck in his motorcycle jacket. She waited, unsure, undecided, in case he crossed the road to her side. Never had her path crossed the path of his kind, never in this kind of direct confrontation. A welter of possibilities came to mind from what little she could see of his face under the yellow-and-blue striped cap.

Oh, that face. That face. Smooth as vanilla or cocoa cream, smooth as those sweet flavors she could lick right off a spoon. A smoothness sharpened by the chill that would have turned paler complexions blotchy red. The color of roasted chestnuts, which she suddenly smelled in the air, the two sensations merging indelibly in her mind: the skin of Cub, the smell of chestnuts. Dark and murky and unreadable eyes with an odd gleam of gold as if spangled with flecks visible only at a particular angle. Mary, who was now past seventy-five, gazed upon a beauty that cut to her core and shook her as if she were still fifteen; and this beauty was contained in a small Jamaican boy who couldn't have been more than thirteen and who, with his hands in his pockets and his gum in his mouth, was watching her house for some reason she didn't want, at least just yet, to guess.

It was she who finally ended up crossing the street. She walked up and stood in front of him. The boy's eyes, glancing far too quickly over her, indicated nothing. He held out his hand and said, "Good morning, ma'am," and, unthinkingly, she shook it. It wasn't a routine gesture of meeting: the two palms touched, the thumbs crossed one another, a momentary and almost imperceptible handshake. Mary turned the boy's hand just enough to set it above hers, his palm facing downward, and Mary's thumb, ever so gently, stroked it, seeking out that warm haze that she had just seen on his face.

He said nothing, did nothing. He waited as if he had all the time in the world. There might have been some hidden contempt in his eyes for everything she represented, everything that was unfamiliar to him. But his gaze shifted downward to their hands together. And so she saw what he was looking at: their difference.

When she finally let go, he nodded—knowingly? pityingly?—and asked her if she needed someone for odd jobs. "Like fixing this window," he murmured. "No," she said, then: "Yes." And, undecided, a bit lost, she suggested that he come back the next day. With that, she left, shaky, pale, stupidly happy, having forgotten what it was she meant to buy, but what did it matter, what did it matter, she had just witnessed true beauty.

Mary walked without seeing anything, without any real understanding of the wholly extraordinary tenderness swelling within her for this boy whose world was so unlike her own.

She had never had children, and so she had scarcely imagined that she might ever hold someone's hand in this way: deferentially. Neither of them had been in a hurry to let go. She had gripped this little hand and felt the texture of warm clay again, solid yet malleable, a completeness she hadn't felt since her ailments had contorted her fingers.

For a moment, Mary was scared of herself. No, she said, don't go there, he has nothing to do with you, there's no space for him in your life . . . But the truth was that there was far too much space in her life, too many rooms to fill. She was past seventy-five, her hands were practically paralyzed, she could no longer bear this loneliness nor this emptiness. She would rather that her final years, or months, or weeks, or days, or hours be shared. But with whom? Or what? The thoughts flowed past her and she was astonished to find herself thinking that, if he came back tomorrow, she would bake him a lemon cake, not too much sugar, slightly bitter, and he'd dip a slice in his tea before letting it melt in his mouth.

But did he like lemon cake? What did kids eat these days? She looked around, stupefied. Saw a McDonald's, a kebab stand, an Indian restaurant, a wine bar, a Starbucks. She walked into the coffee shop and contemplated the American desserts, the brownies, the cookies, the enormous muffins and the endless varieties of coffee with incomprehensible names.

No mirabelle tarts, she realized. I never did learn how to make them.

The fact that she'd never stopped thinking about Howard made her smile. Her memory of Howard had been such a constant presence in her life that she had never felt lonely. There had always been someone beside her, in the living room, in the kitchen, in her bed, even fleetingly, intangibly. But after this encounter with that boy, she had to accept the fact that Howard had no substance. The energy that child had exuded, the solidity of his flesh, his muscles, his lips, left her with the reality that Howard was nothing more than a ghost. This boy was the opposite: an incarnation of Mary's clay statuettes, but far heavier, far more pliable, far more changeable, far more—the word astonished her—erotic.

Mary staggered down Portobello Road, oblivious to everyone around her, unresponsive to their friendly hellos. The vertigo that had just overcome her was so strong she was terrified of collapsing on the pavement. Somehow she managed to continue walking, her fingers clenching the thick fabric of her coat. She stepped into a bookshop and found a cookbook. It was only when she got to the till that she saw that it cost twenty pounds. She didn't have that sum, and, with an apology, she left it on the counter and walked out of the shop. As she stood outside, she looked around and saw that everything had changed: a will to live blazed from every corner of the city, a will that was taking root within her.

Cub didn't know why he was watching this house on Portobello Road. He had ended up there at random. He stared at the open window. Why was he staring at the open window? What did he imagine was behind those walls? It was curiosity, he thought to himself, just morbid curiosity that had made him stop and examine this old woman's residence reeking of damp, archaic dust, or maybe it was because one of his friends had pointed it out the night before and said, "See that house? There's some crazy old hag there, and the place is worth millions." Millions . . . Cub didn't really believe it, although maybe the others, in better shape with fresh coats of paint and elegant curtains, could fetch a sum like that—but this one, more gray than white, with shutters that had once been yellow but were now closer to the color of urine, and the square of muddy earth where a few withered bushes held out against the weeds and the rubbish that passersby had thrown thoughtlessly, no, it couldn't ever be worth that much, but all the same, that woman, maybe she was rich, maybe she needed company . . .

Then she had come out, and in the space of a single instant he had seen her face, blurred by old age into something unremarkable, something forgettable, transform. It was as if his presence had sparked a light within her. He had felt an unfamiliar sadness as he saw the weight of her loneliness, like a white shadow draped over her shoulders. He explained himself by talking about work he could do, and she took him at his word, she told him to come back the next day, and this short conversation had taken place as she'd held his hand and stroked it gently with her thumb. Another conversation, a silent one, had played out between their two hands.

The next day, when he remembered her, the recollection caught him by surprise. He'd hung out with the gang, smoked a joint with them, turned down some crack because he didn't have any money and also because his mother would have killed him straightaway if she ever found out that he'd had some. He'd gone back to the house and fixed his brother Toothpick's scooter, since Toothpick somehow managed to break everything he laid hands on. A day like any other, lazy but full, with an odd aftertaste of bitterness and incompleteness.

It was only as he was getting ready to head out later that evening that he remembered the old lady. He wondered if he should go to see her, just like that, for no reason, maybe to make sure that the white shadow had been real, maybe with the hope of getting some money out of her, but really for no reason, just because he felt like it. He'd never done anything like that. He'd just been getting on with his own life, his own routine. But for some time now he'd been noticing things, lives being lived right beside his own, thinking about those worlds that never touched, and he wanted to know more. His own life had become too narrow.

He was no longer a child, if he had ever really been

one. His mother, his sisters and his little brother had been like satellites orbiting around him, and he was the sun. He was starting to take measure of his strength. Of his attractiveness. The golden gleam that shone in the eyes of women of all ages, of all races, when they saw him, the gleam that had taken him a while to understand but which now he understood all too well. It was a game he hadn't fathomed at first; now he was starting to figure out the rules. It was a pastime he'd come to enjoy more and more, as he gazed at himself in the mirror through lowered eyelashes, his inscrutable eyes, his lips pouting in a way that made his face even rounder, even fleshier, even more succulent.

He heard high-pitched teenage laughter on the other side of the partition. His sisters. Jasmine and Sondra were probably gossiping about boys at their school or trying on clothes or shoes or joking about girls who weren't as pretty as them. The somewhat pleasant smell of grilled food rose up from the kitchen, even though he knew that it was just the frozen hamburger patties his mother always bought so she wouldn't have to cook. His little brother was trying to do his homework in the bedroom the two of them shared, but he was also browsing the web for some porn: the fatter the women, the harder Toothpick got. In the bathroom, there were always reminders of the girls. Their cosmetic products, their underclothes, their hair-removal creams, their shampoos. Their straightening irons, which they used every morning to smooth out their hair until it fell as straight as black straw down to their shoulders (they hadn't succumbed just yet to the wigs or weaves displayed in the shop windows of Brixton, where they were in demand). Cub couldn't understand why they kept doing such boring things over and over. He couldn't bear the ammonia stench of chemical products and burnt hair. He tried his best not to breathe in their presence, despite their charming features, their radiant bodies that were stirring up dangerous glimmers in his friends' eyes, and their dizzying laughter.

His real name was Jeremiah Phillips. He kept on looking at himself in the mirror, unaware that he was copying his sisters' seductive posture, their hooded gaze, their pout, their enigmatic smile. The girls he walked past in his neighborhood, with their bare midriffs and long legs, weren't who he was thinking of so much as the older, white women in the chic pockets of London, protected by their armor of silver. He saw them in restaurants, their fingers gripping the long thin stem of a champagne glass, their legs caressed by the silky, practically invisible veil of sheer stockings bearing practically no relation to the opaque tights his mother wore, huge leather handbags as supple as cloth and set on the floor by their feet or on a chair next to them. He envied them their elegance, their affluence. Their modulated voices, their discreet accents so unlike the shrill shrieks of the neighborhood girls, whatever their race. He wanted them to notice him and look at him, to look at him and want him, and to know that there would be a price to pay. At night, he dreamed of them, their long curved bodies, their red lips, their pale complexions, their soft genitals. A prince, he thought, I'll be their prince. They'll be kneeling before me. They'll be my way out of Brixton.

He became a man at breakneck speed, and that delighted him. Turmoil churned deep in his belly, tormenting him, filling him with joy as his sex swelled. But with his willowy height and his angelic face, his skin demanding to be caressed, a mouth that sent frissons down the backs of men and women alike, it was his seeming innocence that made him so dangerous.

The smell of something burning reached him well before his mother, Wanda, shouted, "Will one of you turn off that damn oven? I'm on the phone!" His sisters and his brother paid no attention to her words, but Cub, whistling, shook his dreadlocks like a girl, stepped out of the bathroom and went to turn off the oven and throw the charred burgers in the bin.

"Mum!" he shouted. "Can we get some Chinese?"

"Fine! Take the money in my handbag!"

He opened his mother's old handbag and took out a twenty-pound note. Looking at the bag he'd seen nearly all his life, the brown, worn-out plastic, the seams coming apart, the lining torn, he felt a kind of pity. If I get some money, he thought, I'll buy Mum some nicer clothes. And a handbag and shoes. He felt disheartened to be taking so much and not giving anything back. It was time to be a man, he thought.

He peeked into the living room. Wanda was lying on the sofa, holding the phone to her ear. The soles of her feet, propped up on the back of the sofa, were yellow from standing for hours at the supermarket where she worked as a cashier. Management had suddenly decided that the cashiers would have fewer back problems if they stood rather than sat. So all the cashiers' chairs were taken away. But now, at the end of their day, their legs were swollen and their short breaks didn't give them enough time to relax or to lie down. They had weakly protested, but the doctor hired by the company had rubber-stamped the decision. Because they needed this work more than they needed their health, the cashiers had kept quiet, even though every morning they felt like they were being sentenced to forced labor and every night they walked like old women, with small, shaky steps.

Wanda was listening to Bob Marley while talking on the phone. "No Woman, No Cry" reverberated through the flat. While Wanda was saying, despairingly, "If he doesn't pay maintenance this month I'm getting a lawyer!" Bob was chiming in that his feet were his only carriage, that he'd have to push through, but everything would be all right, everything would be all right. Of course.

Cub watched his mother and saw her tightly clenched jaw, her red fingernails, her fiery eyes.

Wanda had always been a fighter; she hadn't given up, even after her man had abandoned her, even with four kids, even with all the money she needed but never had. Still, life kept slipping out of her grasp, age was taking its toll, the shop was wringing its cashiers dry and everything cost more and more. Including her kids. Especially her kids who were growing, who kept on asking for money, and she scowled as she painted her nails crimson because she knew she'd run out of luck, there were no fairies or miracles in store for her. She held on to the flat that she rented at a low rate from the local council, but there, too, the future wasn't on her side. The council was in the process of taking back flats and selling them on at market rate to young professionals all too eager to gentrify decaying corners of London such as Brixton. *Everything's gonna be all right.* Bob Marley had no idea what he was talking about. All the families thrown out on the street because they had the right to low rents even though their flats were worth their weight in gold knew that everything wasn't gonna be all right—far from it, in fact.

Wanda hung up and lit a cigarette. Her eyes met Cub's through the smoke. For half a second, Cub was sure she was about to cry. But Bob Marley sang *Oh little sister, don't shed no tears*, and Wanda's face hardened, and Cub knew this woman wasn't the sort to cry. On the contrary, Wanda smiled and turned up the volume, shrugging regally.

Once Cub was out of the building, he'd made his decision. Wanda wouldn't be alone anymore. His gait changed. Never had he seemed so much like a young lion—a lion Cub with sharp teeth, with a small, metallic fury in his belly that just kept on growing.

"In this bright future," he hummed, pausing briefly to jive before going on his way, "you can't forget your past, so dry your tears, I say."

After he'd brought the Chinese takeaway home, he left again to meet his friends at King's Cross. Then, he told himself, he'd go to see the old lady.

Was that really how it had happened? Mary's memory seemed to have erased the moment when her life began. Should she have gained so much happiness there and then? She tried to reconstruct it, filled with regret that her distraction had robbed her of such sweet, precious moments.

When he came back and rang the bell (or knocked? Did he knock? Or bang?), Mary ought to have looked through the window mistrustfully, since nobody had paid her a visit in such a long time; even the occasional missionaries and salesmen had learned to skip this house where both their prayers and their wares invariably came to naught.

She had come down the stairs, her heart pounding, overcome by a fear she couldn't place even as she ran her hand through her somewhat unkempt hair and smoothed her rumpled old dress, all too aware of how her bones showed through her thin skin. She had decided not to open the door. But she needed to know who had gone to the trouble of climbing the few steps up to the front door when there was nothing to catch a passerby's attention: the window displayed only a few dusty corpses.

At first she hadn't seen anything. Then, lowering her eyes, she must have noticed the yellow-and-blue wool cap perched atop the thick hair, and she recognized the child from the previous evening, and, without expecting it, felt a painful twinge of happiness deep within her bosom, an emotion so forceful that she reeled and had to steady herself on the door handle.

It was him, that child whose hand she'd held, who was now standing in front of the door almost without any expectation. What was this inexplicable new feeling swelling up as she turned the lock, almost frenetically, and opened the door? They stood immobile for several seconds, facing each other, as she urged her heart to stop pounding so wildly and tried to regain the breath his presence had stolen away.

Cub, examining her face, seemed to sense the intensity of her joy. Had he realized that his return to the house was a miracle she hadn't dared hope for?

She led him to the kitchen, asked him if he wanted hot chocolate or orange juice. "Orange juice," he said, and he watched, astonished, as she took a tin of red powder out of the cabinet and poured two spoonfuls into a glass she'd filled with tap water. The water took on an almost purplish tint. She held it out and he nervously sipped a little. As he'd expected, the chemical flavor that filled his mouth was unpleasant. He set down the glass, and then, under Mary's anxious gaze, drank another mouthful.

She babbled about the work that needed to be done on the house. He nodded as if he were a professional handyman even though he'd never changed a single light bulb. But his eyes lingered on the green kitchen cabinets, the worn linoleum, the Formica furniture from another era. He took in the space and realized the extent of her poverty, saw how she was filling the silence between them so as to keep him from leaving.

He wasn't sure what made him decide to stay and eat the disgusting meal she made him. She took a packet of turkey slices that smelled like plastic out of a practically empty refrigerator and added a shocking-green sweet mint jelly the likes of which he'd never tasted before in his life. He swallowed it all unthinkingly and got up to fix the bathroom window with the rusty tools she'd found under the sink. It made him happy to know that he'd succeeded at this first job. In the end, because it had started raining outside, he accepted her offer to sleep in a tiny room that served as a storeroom.

He had no idea what he was doing. He was used to following his instincts. If he had to explain it, he would have told himself that there was enough space here that he'd feel less cramped than at his mother's, and that the quiet was nice. He would have told himself that the old woman would give him more money than his work was worth and that he could finally start helping his mother. He would have told himself that this was the first time someone seemed to need him.

But there wasn't any real explanation. Only an instinct toward life and maybe toward death, only the gleam that had shone in Mary's eyes when she had opened the door, only the feeling of a single-minded process that neither she nor he had the power to alter.

He spent the night in Mary's house and, despite the smallness of the room, he slept well. He wasn't awoken by angry women yelling at drunken men, or by wailing babies, or by fists pounding on walls, or even by the brief, mortal blast of a firearm. Nothing of the sort happened on Portobello Road. This almost-unreal calm amazed him. When he woke up early, with the damp, weak light filtering through a small window high up, he lay outstretched on his mattress and realized that this was the first time in his life that he had slept alone.

Later that day, as he got ready to leave, Mary asked him if he would return that night. He said yes without even considering it. And so he did. The days became weeks. Cub was always there.

Mary, wild with joy, went out to discover the color of her city.

The sonorous, luminous, blossoming gleam of the large parks amid a world of chaotic hives and night-time bursts of steam. The metallic, cold sheen of the City where everything was tallied up and calculated in the guise of rigid conformity, where billions were traded away and, in a single second, with the tap of a keyboard button, the futures of the poorest were ground down to rubble. The weathered, jaundiced, gray glare of the suburbs, houses arrayed in their gloom, united in their ugliness, shoulder-to-shoulder in their determination not to fall, practically imprisoning their inhabitants with their lifetimes of debt, sentencing them to dreary streets that nobody explored anymore. The face of the run-down areas, where the dregs of humanity sucked on whatever they could to extract the sticky, mind-numbing substance that substituted for life.

When she was young, there were basement rooms where the only horizon that could be seen was the feet of people walking by outside. They had nowhere to go. Sometimes those feet had looked like those of stocky animals ready to stomp their souls flat. Babies were born already suffused by the damp that never disappeared from the city. They grew up spongy and died spongy, the women with swollen ankles, the men with bloated bellies.

As Mary tried to craft a life on Portobello Road and as she focused her energy on clay, her thoughts overwhelmed at every moment by Howard, the world she had known vanished. Half a century faded in her blurring eyesight, in her aching hands. She hadn't seen these changes happening, but when she opened her eyes again, the horizon itself had changed.

She had believed that she could go on as she had before, because she lived in a bubble where the transformation wasn't so total just yet. And, in this street, the past remained stubbornly alive. The skyscrapers still seemed distant. She didn't realize that the devastation wrought on her face, her body, her increasingly unsure fingers meant it was too late for her to nurture other hopes.

Poverty, too, had taken on other guises, and tried to hide itself behind mobile phones, massive television screens, dazzling cars that conjured up a fog of illusions all too easily shattered. Nobody let their misery show through. But the creases around their eyes and mouths betrayed them, the fissures that opened up at the smallest failure. They clung by their fingertips to the edge of survival.

Mary walked down these streets, convinced she was dreaming. She didn't consider herself part of such an ordinary reality because it seemed inconceivable that anyone could go on living there. And she wasn't walking so much as she was haunting this city. Ever since she had met Cub, she had gone looking for him everywhere. He had burst into her life and left so many questions in his wake. Where had he come from, what was beneath that dark skin, what had his past been like, what did his future hold? Cub was an incandescent presence in Mary's house, but he seemed to have come from nowhere, as if he had been created out of nothing with no obligation to anyone, or had come out of some fantasy Mary had unwittingly nourished. From the moment he had appeared, it had seemed inconceivable to Mary that he might not have existed. He had always been there. He would always be there. And she had to have him, all of him.

He had opened the shutters of her mind and her body; the light that shone through was as unsettling as it was devastating. Because that light was above all a condemnation. Like the house itself, Mary had believed that she was graceless, and that she was long past the point of no return. But Cub had shaken her resignation: he would be her oxygen.

And for that reason, in order not to lose the smallest bit of him, she had gone out to see where he lived. She had done her research. She had dug up his address. She had the audacity to go to Brixton and had followed him to the Hillside Estate, where she had gazed, her mouth agape, her head raised up, at those immense blocks of concrete poured in the sixties as if to close off the sky and the space, where thousands of people were piled up and silence was no more. She had seen, at a distance, his mother, his brother and sisters, the void of a nonexistent father, the worry and suspicion inherent in those who have grown up in a space that would always, in their eyes, be usurped.

It was the first time she'd entered this world. Mary's

England had stayed monochromatic for so long. Only now was she taking stock of the incredible range of hues visible around her. She could have been on another planet. She had never felt any need to take that necessary step toward those who had populated her city without her noticing, not by choice but because the walls of her life had hidden them so efficiently.

She had crossed a boundary and was now somewhere else. She discovered pockets, open spaces that each group had appropriated and where she felt like an intruder. The pointed glares and closed-off expressions were a stern warning that she ignored anyway with a courage that astonished her. Even the aromas changed: guavas, paprika, smoked meat, dried fish, blaring music, rose and orange blossom extract, the detritus of joints from who knew where, bits and pieces of civilization thrown in a bag and mixed together energetically without actually combining them, violence clashing against violence, these momentary alliances engendering dizziness—the foreigner she was entered at her risk and at her peril. The noises and colors assailed her as well, from reggae to rap, rock to bhangra, as she walked down High Street, and the faces and clothes seemed equally covered with floral and tropical patterns, except for when she walked past a veiled woman floating by in silence.

In spite of the fear that seized her as she got on the 159 bus, she kept going. She followed a group of women to the local market, watched what they were buying and picked up the same things: plantains, chayotes, yams, pili-pili, dried prawns, coconut milk, and copied their way of weighing the vegetables, checking their thickness and firmness, holding a melon up to her nose to inhale its scent while squinting. When it was time for her to pay, she reached into her wallet for her savings. But this was for Cub, this was her way of keeping him near and making sure he wouldn't disappear as quickly as he'd arrived, and she went home with her purchases, her arms over-extended, her fingers wrenched in pain, her palm cut in half by the heavy plastic bags, feeling a new sympathy for those women who had shown her the other side of life, Cub's life.

She came home, her back hunched from their distrustful stares, and tried to prepare a meal Cub might have eaten, unaware that he never ate fried plantain or paprika chicken, that he subsisted on endless burgers that he gulped down mindlessly, and that his mother had no idea how to cook those things either because nobody had ever taught her.

Cub greeted these pathetic attempts with indifference, with the strange silence so characteristic of him. He ate a spoonful because she begged him to, won't you please, sweetheart, you need to grow: he swallowed without tasting. Then he went out, as he always did, without telling her where he was going. Sitting alone at the kitchen table, she finished the rest, ate the last crumbs off Cub's plate, ate with his fork as if in a way she wanted to swallow him as well and keep him within her, entirely inside her, never to let him escape ever. But her fragile stomach could not tolerate any of these heavily spiced dishes and, much later, seized by waves of indigestion, she contorted with pain in her bed.

One night, he came in and saw her on the landing, bent in half by those spasms. He helped her to get up and took her to her bed. He brought her a cup of hot tea that he slowly, gently made her drink. He sat on the edge of her bed and stroked her forehead paternally.

He was astonished by her weakness: he was used to warriors in his neighborhood, where nobody would go down without a fight. His mother, even though she looked so frail, would never concede defeat even if she was threatened with eviction for not paying rent. So much weakness for no reason, he thought as he watched Mary. Life didn't seem to have done anything to her, didn't seem to have taken anything away. She alone didn't know what to do or what to make of life. And she was crying about that.

A part of Cub understood that this wound had been born out of solitude and abandonment.

But the man deep within him sneered in disdain, even as he watched this pathetic, trembling, suffering thing under her listless sheets. He understood that he was holding this fragile life in his hands. He could, if he wanted, hold a pillow down over her face and she would be powerless to defend herself. But he could give her a momentary respite, as if he were a deity overflowing with gifts and miracles. He wavered between these two impulses that he barely understood, and he decided to offer her life. He reached out and, overcoming a brief surge of disgust, caressed her unruly, thinning hair damp with fever. A sort of childish delight bathed Mary's face. The suffering drained away from her eyes. In a second, Cub had erased her distress and her fear. He shivered at his power.

He wanted to return to the small room where he slept, but she gripped his hand. Her tears started flowing again, silent and abundant, down both sides of her face. She wanted to immerse herself utterly in the presence of this child's strong, vibrant body. She drank in his vigor, inhaled the fiery energy he exuded. No matter why he was there. He had granted her a reprieve. She who was just a shadow, who had lived so little. She who was so, so cold. A sun, a flame, an incandescence, blazing out of the nothingness all around her. Having experienced this, she couldn't let him go.

She squeezed his hand again and tugged him nearer. He let himself be pulled close. He lay beside her and let her draw his body against hers, right up against hers, so that the pain would pass.

Mary smiled in happiness, but there was no telling what Cub felt. Maybe even he himself didn't know.

It was raining relentlessly. It never stopped raining. The humidity clung to the ceiling, dripped into the bowls she was forced to place in the middle of each room, eroding the walls from beneath. The house seemed about to collapse on her. But her body, too, worn down by old age, seemed about to collapse. Who *was* she? A core, a heart, a belly? What in her suggested that she might still be alive if not the beating of her heart, and the need to fill this belly, to evacuate it? Nothing more, nothing beyond these functions that barely distinguished her from an animal.

All around her the empty days were scattered and strewn. She stared at them, but to no avail: nothing differentiated them, except for Cub's presence. Even if he didn't seem to want to go, he wasn't really there, he went out and came back at any hour he liked, she never knew where he was going. She didn't have any hold on him. Nobody, clearly, had any hold on him. He was the most elusive of creatures even though she would do anything she could to keep him.

Ever since the night she had held on to his hand, he had slept in her bedroom, in her bed.

They hadn't talked about it, they hadn't said anything about it to each other. Cub accepted everything in a silence that did not brook any interruption. Mary could not figure out why he had a lost look when he woke up in the morning. He looked around, touched the sheets and his skin as if to make sure that he did exist. She, too, knew that she had willingly forgotten something about him, that she was repressing a truth in her mind and in her senses, and because of that they had become buoys for one another.

Their sleep was tormented, their bodies dozed in turmoil. They traveled through bitter dreams they didn't dare put into words.

Whenever Cub left the house, Mary watched him through the bedroom window. She contemplated the harmony of his body, the tongues of light licking at his cheek and back, and the sort of transparency that set him apart from everything. She watched him leaving as if it were for the final time. She imagined that he would never come back. She knew she wouldn't survive it. He couldn't leave, she thought.

And it was just then, when she found herself all alone, that all the mockery of the city, her city, of everybody and everything that had abandoned her, came back. Oh, how much she had loved living there when she was young! She tasted a freedom that her mother had never experienced, joined in the wild dance of the city until she had internalized everything: the sellers and the buyers on Portobello Road, the regulars and the tourists, the curious and the obsessed, the connoisseurs and the dilettantes, she mingled with them all, she belonged to them all. She had believed that her hands' work had given her feet the right to join in their dance. She had believed that she, too, was at the heart of things, but she hadn't realized, amid so many relics, that she was growing older and older as wave after new wave of passersby swept past outside.

Mary only became afraid of her old age once it had fully arrived, settling on her body like the Old Man of the Sea on Sinbad's shoulders. It grew heavier and heavier, but casting it off would mean dying.

Heat, it was heat she kept looking for. She'd always been so cold, so cold deep down, trapped in a polar, unvaryingly white world. Her nose was red, her extremities icy; she set her feet on the boiling radiators and felt nothing, nothing at all, she set her eyes on the world's blazing things and felt nothing, nothing at all. She knew this cold was coming from somewhere else, it wasn't the air that struck her face when she opened the door in the mornings, but rather the sigh the city was exhaling. It was possible to love this city and suffer from it at the same time. It was possible to look for streaks of sunlight crisscrossing windows, to walk down its streets with almond trees blooming in the spring, to disappear into the rose garden at Regent's Park, but every adventure ended with the same realization: the city made itself beautiful, dressed itself up in its finery and opera and pealing bells and its preposterous coronet of sunshine, only for those who were swept up in its ascent. Everyone else, stuck in the mud and unable to move, saw nothing but dirt and disdain.

It was possible to love this city and die of it.

To love its hidden stars and its cemented sky.

To love its children who laughed in Leicester Square and who experienced life so immediately that nothing of it remained in their memories. Each night, the same ritual that drove them to disappear into their tenth pint of beer, to sink into their incessant drunkenness, the girls with bare shoulders and midriffs even in the middle of winter because alcohol had lined their insides with false warmth, the boys with distressed jeans and brand-name trainers barely looking at them while they kissed.

To love the old folks dying in Stockwell, sitting on a bench, while the houses they'd bought and lived in for so long became luxury residences for the nouveau riche. No more space, no more space, except for the conquerors. The City rose up and up and up. The town stretched out and swallowed up those who couldn't swim. It waged its own war, the young gods sitting astride it to collect their spoils, to take everything that could be taken, their mouths wide open to seize the air, the wind, the weather, life itself, groans of destruction, of construction, and meanwhile the invisible ones were crushed in the iron jaws.

Waiting for Cub to come back from whatever trip he'd taken into the city, Mary turned on the television to mask the silence of his absence. On the BBC, a woman was barking insults at the players on a quiz show. Her arrogance and her snideness were so brutal that Mary shivered for the contestants as she trained her small, spiteful eyes on them. She wondered why they were there. Did the excitement of being on TV negate the indignity of being so thoroughly humiliated? She held her breath on behalf of a young girl with a halting voice. She knew what was about to happen. Nothing warranted compassionate silence, not a worn face, or a balding scalp, or a hefty body, or a coarse voice. And the host bore a small, horrid grimace as she spat her venom: halfway between scowling and baring her teeth, she resembled nothing so much as a cruel ape. Mary was as hypnotized as a prey confronted by its predator. Then she remembered that she wasn't the prey here: within her fingers, she held freedom. She pressed the remote-control button and let silence reestablish its domain. The pain of absence, at least, was properly hers.

The rain had stopped. Mary noticed the crystalline light now slipping into the leaden-gray living room. But, inside, she could still hear water dripping in a bowl.

She got up to see where it was coming from. Her joints were stiff and she had trouble straightening her back. The damp was so deeply rooted within her that she couldn't even imagine a dry world where bodies wouldn't instinctively rebel.

She turned on a dust-furred light bulb that barely had any effect on the shadows on the walls. She looked at the basin that, a bit earlier, had held three inches of rainwater. Now dozens of small worms were floating in the water. And others were falling in with that tiny splash she had heard from the living room.

She watched with morbid fascination as a worm twisted around a hole in the ceiling, crawled through and hung on by some unknown means—suction pads or microscopic claws—before finally falling.

Mary stepped back, one slow step at a time, so she wouldn't make any noise and catch their attention.

She clapped her hand over her mouth. How would she sleep tonight?

She staggered through the doorway, unable to control her limbs, knowing how much she must look like a scarecrow in her padded, flowery night-robe.

In the hallway, she fell, almost literally, on Cub.

"Jeremiah," she said. "Could you . . . Would you . . . I have a problem."

He followed her into the bedroom. As he did every time, he gazed distantly into this old-fashioned, overly formal room, with its relics—there was no other word—of an England that no longer had any part to play in the present. The captive weight of a life once full of certainties that was now completely undone. Each time, as she watched Cub, it was Mary who felt like a stranger. Seeing everything through the boy's eyes, she understood the place for what it really was: the expression of her emptiness, her uselessness. Through Cub's eyes, she understood it all.

"Can you get rid of the bowl?" she asked, suddenly horrified at the thought that he might think she had done her business there in a bout of incontinence. But Cub was inattentive, his eyes glassy and heavy, almost dead, yes, that was the word, and he walked to the bowl without saying anything.

"There are some worms . . ." she whispered.

He scrutinized the water as if from a great distance. He dipped a finger in, touched the odd creatures swimming there, seemed to toy with them incuriously. Then he looked up to the ceiling.

"Maybe an animal died up there . . ." he whispered. "Or somebody . . ."

Mary slumped against the door. "Oh, dear lord, no, no . . ."

She thought she could see a corpse dripping tears of putrefaction, enveloping her with its stench. Soon it would engulf the entire house, the building, the street, Portobello Road and all its antiques, this past that was now useless— this past that she had wrongly presumed enduring.

Mary gagged again, stopped herself from screaming. She saw Cub staring at her oddly. His eyes were coated in a black film. He was unreadable while she became more and more transparent.

"Should I pour the water down the toilet?" he finally asked.

"No, please, not here . . ."

(And at night they would climb out by the dozens and the hundreds, up the smooth porcelain until they over-flowed and fell onto the floor and kept making their way toward her . . .)

"Could you throw them out the back? Behind the rub-bish bins? And then, Jeremiah, if you could be so good as to buy a very strong pesticide . . ."

"All right. Don't worry, I'll take care of it."

She couldn't understand his calmness, his grown-up's patience. He wasn't a child. This little brown thing was a man in disguise. Did she have any idea who he was, what he really wanted? How could she have let him slip so quickly, so wholly, into her life? She pressed her back against the wall in fear.

"Mary . . ." he said.

His voice hadn't deepened fully yet. She caught herself, chided herself: those were stupid fears.

She took two steps, avoiding the space under the hole, knelt down, pulled an old suitcase out from under the bed and removed a brown envelope. She extracted a wrinkled five-pound note, resisting the urge to check how much remained of her savings. How much longer would this last her? How much longer would she live?

In the wardrobe mirror, she saw herself, as wobbly as a clumsy child. Behind her was a small brown thing that was solid, vibrant, extraordinarily graceful. She was on her knees. He watched over her like a lord.

There is no end of it, the voiceless wailing,
No end to the withering of withered flowers,
To the movement of pain that is painless and motionless,
To the drift of the sea and the drifting wreckage,
The bone's prayer to Death its God. . . .

—T. S. ELIOT, *Four Quartets: The Dry Salvages*

She was alone alone too too too much solitude in this city it's unbearable it wears you out it chews you up it runs you down and you never stop looking out at the horizon a friendly gaze but there isn't one or rather they're flowing like strings like ropes like knots have to get up on a chair to grab the knot of solitude and slip it right there and wait for something to knock you down, but what, maybe the last bit of work your hands petrified by cold and pain made, maybe the door shut every time Cub leaves with the fear that he might not come back and the echoes of his footsteps for a long long while even when he's gone, or maybe the mornings when he watches over you and as you wake up the sole glimmer of day slips through but there's no point thinking about it because Cub

    Cub

        Cub

Mary was on her knees and her hoarse sobbing was nothing like laughing or crying. The floorboard was sloping. She would slip, that was for sure. And her hands frozen in grotesque positions could not clutch anything. Her hands frozen over nothingness. Her hands which had assured her survival and which no longer could.

She walked down Portobello Road and the noise was not a noise but a yowling in her cloistered mind. It was market day and the stalls were bustling, the sellers smiling as if life didn't cost a thing. They all flowed together in a motley, blurry crowd beneath her gaze, copper pots blackened by burning wood, objects so oddly gray that there was no question time alone could have formed this patina, sphinxes or four-legged birds with ornate ringlets from a tomb broken open out of sheer curiosity, wooden furniture in all shades battered by the centuries, wooden frames around cracked or wholly missing mirrors that now circumscribed reflections of nothing, faded cloths, heavy brocades that had once whispered their melodies around female forms, a long litany of voices, dreams, refrains, and then paintings, there were so many, so many, the smaller and darker they were, tortured by these immense frames that seemed to entrap gazes, the greater the chance that they were truly old, but who could possibly want these tiny things, these narrowed nighttime visions of clouds over ponds, meadows beneath horses, Brocéliande forests, impossible mountains, or perhaps austere, melancholy portraits of people with ridiculously high foreheads? Not she who would rather make these timeless figurines, even when they were imperfect, than surround herself with these faces that always sneered at you from the hereafter, reminding you that you were just a little thing taking up some air and some space; not she who had poured her love into her statuettes for so long and who now had to accept this prohibition of her sole consolation: all Portobello Road could offer her now was a breath of life, and even that was growing increasingly vengeful and unforgiving.

Even so, the street's spell still had a hold on her, because here the past was always alive, always present in the thousands of objects stolen out of time, the yellowed doilies, the dented forks, the porcelain dolls, how many hands, how many hearts, how many bodies had been touched by them, and their dust remained through the centuries, nothing could be wiped away, maybe that was the true consolation—nothing could be wiped away? And so, as she disappeared, her shadow lingered on the sidewalk, in the heavy gaze of the sellers who watched the world changing every day and in the air ruined by so many smells, and maybe even in her figurines which she could still half see sometimes, as if nearly lost in the immensities of time despite being more present, doubtless more permanent than she ever would be.

For some time now, despite their outward friendliness, people had been regarding the city with warier eyes. She remembered the turmoil of the war and the difficulties after the war clearly enough to consider the era that had followed as a blessed time, even if she herself had stayed on the sidelines. It hardly mattered, since she had lived, she had seen things change, she had seen flowers bloom out of concrete and steel on a ravaged landscape—but, after all those years, the world had collapsed again in a fell swoop.

A huge hole had opened up in the center of the capital. At first rumors had swirled of a far-off war, and she couldn't understand how it might affect her country. What was over there, in those deserted and mythical lands that hadn't been there all along? These weren't wars of ideas or even of territories. These were wars of unclear motives, hidden calculations, like a torrent flowing so deep underground that nobody aboveground could tell which direction the current was. Aboveground, all that mattered was that they believed. Those of the new century were conditioned to believe what they were told.

Two towers had fallen and forced them to believe in the enemy. And especially to believe that this invisible enemy could be overcome in a single place.

The worst thing, in Mary's eyes, was watching the men leave for war. She had watched them, their heads shaven, their eyes serious but barely hiding glimmers of excitement, of hunger, their powerful, gnarled hands, mechanics' hands perhaps, their smart uniforms, their faith above all in something, no matter what name it took, some country or creed, they needed to believe in it because they were being told they were fighting for a cause, and she had seen them go off, those handsome young men, those stupid young men, those dead young men, and it was as if sixty years hadn't gone by between these two wars. And the girls, too, clung to a desperate love, pressing their pliable bodies against the starched uniforms so they would retain the imprint of those fabrics fated to come back as nothing more than shreds. For a minute, in front of the television, Mary really did believe that time had stood still. That she had remained frozen while Howard had gone to get himself killed over there. Her moment of innocence had only lasted a little over half a century.

They heard the same dangerous, cold music beckoning them to their deaths.

A clean war, they said. But hadn't there been bodies rent asunder like bits of cloth on barbed wire? Wasn't human flesh still as easily torn? And didn't these soldiers, these twenty-year-old kids in their algae-tinted fatigues, have the same faces inured to the shock of waking up to the terrible weight of war, the flood of massacres, the sheer human cost?

The truth of this war hit much harder when she saw images on the television of a young American woman soldier humiliating prisoners. The face of this woman shocked her. A murderous, cruel, closed-off child flattened by a total lack of heart or feeling. A face that only saw itself, only saw the small world it had come from, saw the walls as firm as they were invisible, the walls of absolute alienation from the truth of others, the only truth that counted. A sort of tragicomic figure with her absurd poses, her finger pointed at the prisoners forced to masturbate, a grotesque figure of a malefic angel who knew how to dehumanize the enemy so thoroughly that death was merely incidental.

This was the face of the era.

Mary never knew why she cried with rage and impotence as she saw this woman keeping a naked man on a leash, his head covered by a hood.

Mary, at a loss for words, turned toward Cub. But he paid no attention to the war. He paid attention only to his own survival. Mary, having seen where he lived, understood that he was fighting his own war, that after living there, he couldn't be surprised by this surfeit of violence. Cub hadn't looked twice at this soldier woman. He looked a little like her, actually, in spite of his beauty, because of that cold, calculating gaze.

She saw it in his ingenuity in wrangling a few pounds out of her. Never too much, never huge amounts, but it was as if he had punctured a vein with a very thin needle and now Mary's money, droplet by tiny droplet, was escaping.

This was testament to a sort of deep-rooted indifference in which compassion was nowhere to be found.

And so he said one day that he needed to buy some medicine for his mother. She had followed him as she usually did without his realizing it (he never rushed, he wandered as if he had all the time in the world). He bought a beautiful leather handbag. Mary thought, momentarily, that it might be for her, and her cheeks reddened with joy. When he left the shop and got on the 159 bus, a horrible jealousy overcame her. She took the same bus, barely concerned about being seen; his ears were covered by his headphones and his eyes were faraway, he didn't even notice when she walked right in front of him to take a seat behind. For the whole journey, she watched the nape of his neck, so smooth and fragile under his huge hat, his shoulders which rose and fell slightly in rhythm with the unintelligible music he was listening to, his not-so-child-like back. Her jealousy didn't abate in the least as he went straight to his mother's. She took the elevator, indifferent to the obscene graffiti, the stench of urine, the pointed stares that followed her. She was fixated on the footsteps of the one person who mattered. She watched him go into the flat. He left the door ajar. She hid behind the door and watched him offer his mother the handbag.

His mother smiled. This weary woman's smile transformed her face. The dimples in her cheeks deepened, making her look so much younger she seemed like a child. She clutched Cub in her arms, pressed her nose into his hat perched on top of his hair. Mary waited for Cub to pull away quickly, but he stayed there, his eyes less distant, with a smile not unlike his mother's, the same dimples deep in his cheeks. Wanda slung the handbag on her shoulder and swanned like a model. Cub lay down and stretched out across the sofa, crossing his arms behind his head and smiling as he watched his mother simpering.

Mary stepped back, her body as heavy as her heart. Why couldn't she ever have a love like that?

When Cub came back, much later, he was soaked from the rain. Mary ushered him in with exclamations, went to find a towel, and rubbed his head, getting a small sense of this mass of soft, spongy hair. She made him take off his T-shirt and dried off his torso. Her hands slid across his skin and lingered. He did not protest. She wanted to hold him tight against her, but that image of his mother and the smile they had shared held her back. She held this body as long as she could in her hands, and he, as if world-weary, did not pull away.

She ignored the warnings that sapped her spirits. His innocence had no price, she insisted to herself.

Such innocence that he never asked anything about the life the two of them were now living together—that was what she thought, trying to convince herself that Cub knew nothing of this world, even though, of course, he knew this world far better than she did. She didn't dare to step over the threshold into the unknown. He was here. That was enough. But why? What was his intent? She did not want to know.

When he disappeared, she simply waited for him. Between the moment he left and the moment he returned, everything she did was for him. She didn't ask how this story would end, because it never could. Her days crumbled so quickly that she could not be scared of the future: it didn't exist. What about his future? a single, tiny voice asked. What's in store?

If he ever took the time to listen to this voice, if he could have answered it, he would have said that she was wrong, that he had never been innocent because people like him were born all-knowing, with resourcefulness flowing through their veins, their hands closing hungrily on the warmth of life. They had nothing to do with innocence. That was just another word for foolishness. Cub would rather know everything. He had seen murders and rapes, and he had not looked away. Battered children and corpses. He refused to be willfully blind.

In the imaginary conversation the two of them had, he said to her: I am a survivor, that's how people make it. This city doesn't do anything for people like me when we're sentenced from the outset. Every day I meet the lifeless gaze of those who have given up the struggle, those who don't even have the time to get their things before the police kick them out, those the world wants to erase because they're of no use. I am one of those who charge forward right away, who won't be stopped, not even by the walls they build around us or the pits they fill with the bodies of those who tried to cross them. I don't want to cross them. I want to stay on my side of the void and look down from there at you all, dare you all to come join me. I'll dance on my side of the void and you won't be able to touch me.

But Cub did not say those words because he barely talked. Each day he erased himself more and more, pushing himself closer and closer to transparency.

Cub, Cub, Mary said, you're dancing with the sun, your path is toward the others, you're a bridge, a link, you have to change what can be changed. Mary wanted to believe that there was a reason for their meeting.

I don't want to change anything at all and I definitely don't want to be a bridge, Cub said. All I'd do is piss on everybody walking below.

So why are you here? What are you doing here? Mary did not ask those questions. The mere thought that Cub might decide to leave one day tore at her guts and left her reeling. She would do anything to keep that day from coming. She was ready to fight death itself.

Like a madwoman in pursuit of her shadow, she followed him, bumping into strangers, anti-war protesters, pro-war protesters, policemen, dogs, drunkards in search of some warmth, endlessly curious children, endlessly incurious women. She didn't belong in any of their ranks; this world wasn't her own. How many people were there like this, walking around in this city and refusing its embrace? Their path was lonely and the city could have gone under overnight, razed by a bomb, struck by a meteorite, buried by an earthquake, and they wouldn't have noticed. The city was an incubator, it allowed them to exist, but it had formed no bonds of loyalty or of cordiality with them. They were the termites living in its wood, chewing away at its flesh and turning it to dust, but it didn't help them to survive either. They took as good as they got.

Mary followed Cub, who was dancing on a tightrope, dancing for so long so long even with the only music that of his heartbeat, even with his head befuddled by his own hustle and bustle. She only followed his path so she wouldn't lose him, so she'd always know where he was and where he was headed.

Sometimes Cub seemed to be nothing more than the interplay of light in her eyes, sometimes here, sometimes gone, but which he alone imbued with weight.

Where was he going? To tread all the paths, all the routes, all the intersections. Not to lose his way. Never to lose sight of his shadow, never ever. He was the one who experienced miracles. Oh, gods, was such a love even possible? Would such lightning ever strike her?

One Sunday, walking down a street forking off Portobello Road, Mary heard the sounds of a party from the house of one of the shop owners, an Indian man she knew well.

She stopped in front of the place, which was decked out in multicolored lights. Booming music shook the glass panes. The garden was already packed and the hullabaloo just kept growing recklessly. "The flowers here," someone yelled, "no, not there, I said here, no, that huge vase is going to block the door, everyone's going to trip over it, and what's this table doing here? All the tables go in the great hall, and where did the champagne flutes go, aren't there any, the caterer was supposed to bring them, call him, we'll have to buy some and . . ."

The voice was swallowed up by its own hysteria.

From the other side of the street, she sniffed and inhaled all the familiar odors: cumin, sandalwood and asafetida. She smiled at the sheer number of luxury cars from manufacturers she'd never heard of, parked along the sidewalk. She smiled as she saw the steely, resentful glares of the born-and-bred Britons glancing at this display, then, lowering their eyes, hurrying along with their purchases from the corner shop. That evening, as they chewed their bland cold meats, they would hear the sounds of partying and the clinks of crystal coming from the smartest house on the street, the only one not to have been carved up into flats, and they would mull over dreams of elbowing everybody else out.

A long, ostentatious line of cars went down the street. The first, a white limousine, was adorned with flowers, ribbons and silver paper. Those following behind were honking to announce the bridegroom's arrival. Mary saw a pudgy face in the first car, kohl-rimmed eyes, pursed lips. His elbow was perched on the ledge of the open window, the cream-colored silk of his jacket gleaming softly, the sleeve just short enough to reveal a gold Rolex and, on a chubby finger, a sparkling diamond.

More neighbors came out to see what was going on. Some smiled at this riot of color and noise; others scowled and slammed their doors shut and turned up the volume on their TVs. Kids were staring in fascination while teenagers giggled, sorely tempted to stick their gum on the immaculate surfaces. The bare branches on the trees were trembling. A few last leaves fell, and their dance down to the sidewalk reminded Mary that she was cold. Cold, above all, because she was there, contemplating the sounds of this party she had no part in.

An old man made his way out of the house. He had a frayed wool scarf around his head. She realized he was Nari, the owner of the house and of the shop facing Portobello Road on the other side. He saw her and smiled.

"Hello, Mary, did you come for the carnival?"

He seemed to be trying to escape from his own home.

"It's my granddaughter who's getting married," he said. "But I'm not going to stay for the party. They can't make me. What's the point in going over the top like this?

I can't even guess how many millions these cars have to be worth. You know I'd never say no to money, but I haven't got a thing in common with these gazillionaires. Half the ladies in there are even more gussied up than the Taj Mahal! And I'm just thinking about the towers of silence again. I've decided this is it, I'm not going to any more weddings, not even for my family. I'm going to think about towers of silence."

"Towers of silence?" Mary asked. "What are those?"

"An environmentally friendly way of getting rid of the dead," he replied. "Parsis cannot bury or cremate their dead. Thus spake Zarathustra, or Zoroaster, our prophet. So we have to build granite towers, and at the top there are open platforms with hundreds of compartments in concentric rings. The outer circle holds men's bodies, then in the center are the women's bodies, and children's bodies are in the innermost one. Criminals' corpses go somewhere else, on top of a bare cement tower with no decorations. When we die, men dressed in white, whose only job is this, will carry our bodies to the top of those towers. Up there, the vultures are waiting, as still as statues. They know we're coming, and they're waiting. When the garden doors open, they take flight and circle over the towers with a hunger that's downright Pavlovian. The vultures may look ugly, but when they fly they're slow and graceful. Any time they see a new corpse, they come by the thousands. They feed on it completely, intimately. They feast and they stuff themselves, but they're always silent, almost out of respect for these mouths that won't ever talk again. They peck out eyes, chew up cheeks, rip open bellies to yank out succulent entrails. When they're no longer hungry, they take flight again, then they return in circles, closing in and in until they land near the corpse once more. And so, over several days, it's eaten: only the bones are left. The wind and the sun dry them and whiten them. When they're clean and white, the corpse carriers come back and walk to the brink of the pit at the center of the tower, and they throw it all to the bottom, where the bones of the Parsis have been piling up and disintegrating for millennia. And the vultures go on circling around those towers of silence without a single sound. Out of respect for the dead who nourish them."

Nari's face had clouded over again.

"There aren't any towers here, though," he said. "I asked my children to pay for a trip to Bombay, where all my family is waiting for me in the towers of silence. I want to follow in their footsteps and give my body to the vultures who will clean it and purify it. Then I can lie upon them, I can add my calm bones to their sleep. I'll be at peace."

He gave Mary a sad smile.

"Off you go now, don't waste another second thinking about these happy fools," he said. "Or just look at their eyes. You can see how useless they are. They're trapped like flies in their spider web of identity. Here, they're Indians mimicking all the pomp and circumstance of their homeland. In their homeland they're civilized Westerners with too much money, sneering at their compatriots' customs. At heart, they never stop going back and forth; they're lost and alone. All this noise and toasting won't fill the emptiness in their souls. Go home, Mary. Pour yourself a single-malt whisky like me, and get some sleep. You're best off doing that."

"But you miss your towers . . ." Mary replied.

"In the end, what matters is how you die."

Have you seen the old man

. . . .

Kicking up the paper
With his worn out shoes?

. . . .

Yesterday's paper telling yesterday's news

—RALPH McTELL, "Streets of London"

The worms had stopped raining down into the bowl. But this had been replaced by a stench that increased by the hour, which grew so horrible that Mary wondered whether it would wake up the neighbors and the entire neighborhood. She half expected them to come pounding at her door to complain. But nobody came.

Sitting in her armchair, she examined the hole in the ceiling with stubborn concentration. What *was* up there? It was just a closed-off attic that was reached by a trapdoor in the hallway. Could a dead rat give off such an odor? No, it could only be a human corpse.

A few days earlier, she had seen the headline on the front page of a newspaper: MAN JUMPS TO DEATH SPLATTERING THE GUTTER PRESS. Those words had taken her aback, as she hadn't understood what they meant: a man kills himself by jumping from on high, splashing the tabloids. She'd bought the paper to read the article. It had to do with a man of no fixed address who, according to the people interviewed, had taken refuge in the attic of a house, until he could no longer handle the hunger or the cold. At that point he'd climbed to the top of the Post Office Tower and jumped from the spire. The irony was that he landed on a newspaper kiosk. His blood had splattered over the papers that trumpeted exactly this kind of news. Beggars who knew him said that he'd been a war vet who'd never really integrated back into society. He'd lived in the attics of residential homes, sometimes eaten dead rats.

Mary shuddered at the thought that Howard might have lived like this, abandoned by everybody, eating dead rats. And one day, tired of life, he had . . .

Howard, she said, couldn't you have come to me? I would have welcomed you, taken you in. I'd have been your angel and your savior. That was all I wanted, to be useful, to open my arms and my body to the only man I've truly known. Do you know how many lives you could have given me? One for each year we were apart. One for each day and each hour, Howard, an eternity of lives, my body would have been your house, my flesh your nourishment. Dead rats? Howard, you could have eaten me alive and I would have been overjoyed. I've counted for so little. Life's passed us both by completely. Everything went too fast for us. It used to be the world wouldn't have turned without us, and now it doesn't matter whether or not we're still here.

So quickly, so early, all these men who had fought so hard had become useless. Erased from memory by a history retold too many times, like a photo left in the sun too many months. People had forgotten that those men had been flesh and blood before being reduced to names on monuments or rather, before being reduced to the wives and fathers and mothers and children of names on monuments. Other wars were fought, but none, in this country, bore the pathos of these wars, the ones that Mary and Howard and their parents had endured, wars at their doors, in their bellies, in their minds, in their hunger. Holes in the middle of their town, their city, their heads. Generations wiped away. Who remembered the disgusting bread they'd had to gulp down while trying not to vomit? Or that vile gruel that women cooked in secret, masking their shame with a stiff upper lip? Who remembered those maimed young men who had forgotten how to laugh? Erased, erased so quickly, the page was turned, and Mary had become transparent, Howard a beggar feeding on rats who had jumped from the top of a tower.

Beings like glass, filling in their cracks until the day came when they were told that they weren't worth the cost to their country, and these nocturnal, almost inanimate lives came to believe that they would do best to slip through the gaps between cobblestones. Too expensive to go on living.

London was filled with a nameless, homeless population that lived in its crevices and was no longer of any use.

And so Mary convinced herself that in her attic there had been a homeless man who had died of illness or old age or hunger or any of those other things that killed the poor and didn't have a name. She dreamed up a horrific scenario, but she wasn't afraid. Because the dead man had taken on the face of Howard.

As soon as this possibility occurred to her, the presence in the attic invaded her thoughts. It became as real as Cub, who disappeared for hours on end, leaving her alone with the cadaver. She was astonished to find herself holding her breath, listening to the silence. But what did she hear? A dead body did not make any noise. Should she ask Cub to go and see what was up there? She didn't let herself contemplate the prospect: she didn't want to frighten Cub because he might decide to leave for good. She would have to learn to live with it.

She armed herself with a jar of Vicks and rubbed a bit of the ointment under her nostrils whenever the smell was too strong. But it wasn't the same throughout the day. As if the dead body was only able to communicate through smells. Through a strange, illegible bouquet of stenches. She thought she could make out, in these variations, its sadness or its happiness, its memories and its regrets. She could also perceive something odd, akin to a laugh. Every so often, as if the corpse was expressing, with a little puff of methane, a sort of knowing sympathy. One day, she thought to herself, the process of decomposition will be done and there'll be nothing left but dry bones. Time will do its work. What a shame there aren't any vultures . . . She thought of Nari, and of the cleaned bodies joining the others in the towers, embracing one another for centuries. The offering we each make to the birds, but also to the sun and to the wind. Would Howard have wanted to be set down at the summit of a tower, in a fiery place that respected its dead?

Mary pushed the thought away. She shouldn't get used to this presence. Howard was dead.

What mattered was that Cub did not leave. When she waited, Howard filled up her days. She built him a life, a past, a fall from grace. A fantasy that consoled her about her reality.

One night, she looked up and she thought she saw, in the perfect circle of the hole, the gleam of an eye fixed on her. She wanted to jump out of the bed. But her arms and legs were paralyzed, as if this gaze had imprisoned her.

She felt wholly naked. She told herself that he was ogling her with this green-and-black eye, perfectly fitted to the hole's circumference. Only a dead man could watch an old woman with such lust, she thought angrily. For him, I must represent his desire for life.

An unattainable, envious, jealous desire, even if what remains of me isn't worth the dust that slips out of my nooks and crannies.

Then, thinking that maybe it was Howard there and that he, after all, did have the right to watch her, she relaxed and let the eye invade her.

To please it, so as not to anger it, she raised her hands with great effort and slipped off her nightdress. Her white, transparent body was exposed to the dead man's eye, her lattice of blue veins, her network of varicose veins, her knobbly and painful tendons. Do you like that? she asked him, noticing how odd these words were for her, she who probably had never been liked by anybody. Do you like that? A body that neglected itself, but which summoned up a kind of energy, an unexpected swell. The eye did not respond, did not move, but gleamed all the more brightly.

She ended up falling asleep, feeling as if she were not alone. She dreamed that the corpse melted so completely that it flowed through the hole and entered her without her being able to make the least move to defend herself, and that she was now wanly watching this wedding of old bodies.

In the morning, the eye was gone. Mary barely recognized this body that hadn't slept naked in so long. Around her there were traces of dampness: sweat, tears, oily discharge. The sheets were wet and warm. She saw herself from the outside, a pale ghost haunting her home, of unreal slenderness, with skin so thin that she could have easily dissolved into air.

She was consoled by the thought that Cub hadn't come back that night, then she was worried. Was it possible that he'd come back while she was asleep and, seeing her in that state, had fled in disgust?

In the bathroom mirror, she seemed greenish. That color didn't astonish her, though. It was her true complexion, the tint of all the years spreading from her armpits to cover her body. Like her clothes, her weariness, her perspiration, her urine. Like the cracks that opened up across her skin, here and there, and which did not bleed.

She managed to get dressed without thinking too much about the dead homeless man upstairs—about Howard, whom she still desired, no matter whether he was dead or alive. She thought she could hear the sound of him crumpling newspaper to sleep on or cover himself with, and his voice which, in his sleep, rang out and resounded under the roof with a plaintive tone, and then the cracking of his joints when he got up, and then this way he had of scraping bits of bread that had fallen on the wooden planks to eat them, so as not to waste anything, and then the damp haze of his green eyes.

She should remember that he was dead. She should stop thinking of him. She forbade herself from going up to feed him. If he was dead, he didn't need anything. If he was dead, what she saw would be a vision of the devastation that awaited us all. She didn't need that to know that she only had so much time.

Each night the eye appeared in the hole. All it wanted to do was watch her; what else could it do, after all? She eventually got used to it, and even felt flattered by the attention.

One day, as she got dressed, she came across some minuscule changes in her body. Her breasts, which for eons had only been empty pouches, now seemed a little firmer. Her belly, once concave, had rounded out slightly. She didn't dare to turn around to see her bottom in the mirror, but something, her hand most likely, in its curiosity, told her that there was now a new swell there.

She who had lost all her vanity long ago—if she had ever had any—was surprised to notice these changes with a sort of shameful pleasure.

She had wallowed in the comfortable ugliness of this old age that had freed her from all need for disguise. Her body in its simple truth. She was now aware of this naked gaze that looked her over, of this trap right out of a film concealing a secret that no camera could capture. A pupil withdrawing into infinity, no longer contemplating reality but perceiving the layer of lies that covered every face, every word, every image, every feeling. The sharpness of this gaze punctured the elastic membrane between her past and her future—or what remained of it.

Even though this gaze felt ruthless, she no longer felt as alone. And this presence was enough to give her budding body a sort of new, wispy life, of late, wintry, unlikely blossoming.

Each night that she spent under his gaze brought a new sign of youth in the morning. The creased skin of her arms became newly elastic, and the colors of her face shifted from yellow to pink. Mary Rose would never be beautiful. But what she had learned to accept about herself was at odds with what she was now discovering each day. It was only when this old, faux youth arose in her that she could finally admit to herself that maybe she hadn't been that ugly, or that ordinary. That the young girl Howard had chosen one festive night might not have been a last resort, but a deliberate choice.

And that, precisely, was what persuaded her that the dead man in her attic had to be Howard.

It was, after all, the year of miracles. First had been Cub, and then there was her body renewed by a mysterious presence that no longer seemed so nauseating to her. Why wouldn't Howard be one of these miracles? Howard returned from out of time, from the other side of life, come back to hold out his hand and to be, in his last appearance, the spouse that she had never had, and Cub would be the child the two of them shared, the child that her body would never be young enough to have conceived, the child who would give a direction to her crumbling days?

Everything took on new meaning. In her house on Portobello Road, Mary welcomed these monstrous and marvelous gifts with an overflowing heart. She understood that she had shaped figurines in order to create another world, to open a door to the impossible. When she was no longer able to form them, it was this world that had come to her.

White light folded, sheathed about her, folded.
The new years walk, restoring
Through a bright cloud of tears, the years, restoring
With a new verse the ancient rhyme. Redeem
The time. Redeem
The unread vision in the higher dream

—T. S. ELIOT, "Ash Wednesday"

Mary's welcome was enough to persuade him to come down.

His eyes were exactly the same as those in her nonexistent memory. Green and black, with that cheerful chaos that indicated he had come from the other side of the day. Anything that might matter to the living was, for him, simply the childishness of being. At first, Mary was scared to look at him, to see the path decomposition had carved through his flesh, but Howard was nothing more than a beggar fraying around the edges, certainly unwashed, but hardly disgusting.

When Cub left during the day, he came down from the attic. They had so many things to tell each other. She brightened at the thought that she finally had a companion capable of understanding her. Just when she'd lost all hope. He didn't actually talk, but he was there: present. Not a dream, not a nightmare or a hallucination. He was, specifically, beyond all that, because life took on forms that nobody could have ever expected.

One day, Howard took her by the hand. He wanted to lead her through the streets of London. He wanted to show her what he loved about this city that had killed him. He had lived his final years like an animal, in total destitution, he said, defecating under the bridges or on top of the roofs. He pointed out the gaps along the road and the absences among the people. She could see clearly the holes that the dead left in the lives of the living. She certainly was the only one able to distinguish these grayish, melancholy forms, but she told herself that knowing what they were was a sign of permanence, that nobody ever truly left. The beggar whistled, happy in her presence: *I'll show you something to make you change your mind.*

Change my mind about what? she asked, intrigued. About the need to live? Here, especially, where old age isolates us from an incurious world, since it has nothing to do with us? I don't recognize these roads where I lived so long ago. Now I see both the empty and the full. The emptiness, for example, of the woman selling fake jewelry, each one for two pounds, whose face caked in orange makeup gets more wrinkled every day and who has a smoker's voice, warm and rough. There's a gray rectangle on the ground where she usually sits, and the wind blows colder there.

And farther on, the man hawking christening gowns, lace dresses billowing around absent bodies, pink-white-creamy babies, so fine that they look like drops of milk curdled by honey and bees. He's no more there than she is. And the babies who were once in these gowns? Where are they? What has become of them? Those rounded cheeks, those eyes gleaming with their discoveries had to have been lost to history. Unless they had been the features of people who did help change the world. Mary smiled at the thought that Marie Curie might have once worn a gown and some lace just like the ones here. And radium had been discovered even so!

Those she met now were eyeing her like an alien, chewing gum and forcing her to see the grayish, glutinous paste in their mouths, rolling around their pink tongues. She was in a place where people walked in the haze of others, a place where they slipped in the oil slicks of other people's gazes, where nothing was theirs—not even the air other people were breathing frenetically, not even the wafts of foreign spices, not even one's own body which continued obstinately seizing on whatever life it could.

Her back was hunched by guilt, knowing that every glance underscored the certainty of her uselessness, that as soon as she was gone, someone newer, truer, more deserving, would fill her shoes and this space with no fear of the total indifference she absorbed, she a blotter for the most precious inks of life, she a criminal for being so old yet enjoying forbidden happiness. She kept on walking beside Howard and realized why the city hated her so much. I'm an ever-growling belly that has to be fed, and fed, and fed, she said.

Howard smiled. You're wrong, he replied. We aren't useless. My life smelled like newspaper ink and pulp because I slept on newsprint and used it to stay warm in the winter, but the latest news never haunted my dreams. What did words matter to me? I knew that every kind of paper, from the lowliest tabloid to the most prestigious, spread lies that buried their readers in a placid stupidity. None of them talked about this world of piss and filth that I lived in, about the underside of London. That's where my true friends could be found, until hooch or drugs had wrecked their liver and guts. It was just one of many ways for them to die. Cancer or heart attack or car crash or cirrhosis of the liver: Is any sort of death easier than another?

I came back from the war without a soul. My heart broke in the pits of Dunkirk. The trenches welcomed my dreams just as easily as they did my friends' guts. They carried me out on a stretcher and, despite all the efforts of the nurses—no matter how angelic or surly they were—to fix my body, they weren't able to fix my spirit. I went mad. They let me leave, but I was never able to make my way back to Benton-on-Bent, or to take up my trade as a mechanic, or to reconnect with my family and my friends. I landed on some other planet, and the only ones who could understand me were the veterans who, like me, had been trapped within the eternal night of war.

Mary, I spent years on the streets. I discovered an England that nobody knew: fat women smiling giddily, thin girls sweating scornfully, men who became my brothers, brothers who had been my enemies. I saw the whole gamut, Mary. What all the men had in common was that they were different. There wasn't any general trend. There were only personalities nobody could have guessed they'd had when they were born. I met them all. I lived unnoticed in attics where I heard people living their real lives. My God—what an impoverishment! Do you know how many days and weeks and months I spent listening to the same arguments, the same excuses, the same inanities? Was this what we fought for? Was this why we survived?

One evening, after eating nothing for a whole week and hearing a girl whine about her boyfriend refusing to buy her the latest phone, a teenager shouting at her "clueless" parents, a husband telling his wife he was settling down with someone younger, and then the wallpaper and then the phone and then the old shoes and then and then so on so on so on and all this complaining about not having things that had nothing to do with the emptiness in my stomach, the dizziness in my head, the hopelessness in my mind, the sadness in my heart, I went out, and I climbed to the top of the Post Office Tower—I'd slipped through the barriers and the forbidden areas so many times that I had no trouble getting in this time. The elevator got me higher than the level of London's rooftops, which might as well be the roof of the world. I saw London spread out at my feet, a beautiful city after all, such a beautiful city, built out of wartime stagnation to become a symphony of illumination and jubilation for those who claim this city as their own, but I was on the losing side and the city's beauty didn't console me, didn't signify anything for me, the worst thing for us wasn't the void so much as the surplus of other people: they had all decided that I was an outsider.

That night, I jumped from the top of the Post Office Tower while spreading my wings of newsprint. As I fell, I thought I could see people eating in the restaurant that used to be at the top of the tower, eating food so expensive that it could have fed me for a year or even ten. It could have been wine worth three thousand quid or it could have been piss; I didn't care. Their stomachs weren't any more deserving than mine. Their stomachs weren't digesting food any faster than mine was, and their shit wasn't going to stink any less than mine. If they had just looked and seen me falling on the other side of the glass, they would have understood that their fall would have been every bit as deadly. And just like that, every dish they ordered would have started tasting completely flat, like it was just chewed-up money. The wind was rushing past the tower so hard they were sure it would fall. That's the fate of all towers, after all, to fall. And so I was hurtling headlong, without making a sound. Which was fine, that was how I ended up in the local news with a couple of paragraphs about a bloody explosion. I hadn't read a single word of those papers I had wrapped around myself every night, and there I was all the same: MAN JUMPS TO DEATH SPLATTERING THE GUTTER PRESS. A man in the gutter, that's what I was.

Now, come with me.

Mary took a few more steps. They headed toward the river together. Mary's sadness was immense, deep, territorial. But, as she watched Howard out of the corner of her eye, she was sure she saw colors slipping out of his hands, like the lights that hung around the top of the tower.

He dragged her to the Thames. Her icy feet stumbled in the slippers she'd forgotten to change before heading out. She walked toward the edge of the water, following him down winding paths along the canals and beneath the bridges, paying no attention to the junk and refuse they came across, the boys and girls enveloped in musty odors or stippled with pinpricks, old people who might as well have been dead, young people who might as well have been old, rubbish thrown from the bridge and which testified to that horrible propensity to throw away, to keep on throwing away what could be used, clean sheets of paper, half-eaten food, outdated television screens, broken computers, everything had been thrown out, everything had been abandoned with absolute indifference in a landscape of ugliness, and it seemed almost intentional that nature should only offer brambles and thorns that bristled against all who would enter.

But when she finally reached the river's edge, things

changed. The clouds moved apart to let through a huge outpouring of sunlight. The water responded in kind, saying *Hello, hello, dear* to the sky. Mary was astonished by their mutual gleaming. She froze there, charmed and amazed at the same time. She had the impression that it was Howard who was making the daylight dance.

A barge came through with sharp ululations. Seagulls dive-bombed. The air was tumultuous. The water exuded an unusual warmth. A smile sloshed around her stomach, flipped around like a carp.

She looked straight at the sun, waiting for it to descend. The few people strolling nearby, all too aware of the river's treacherous coldness, lingered in fascination. They, too, seemed captivated. They even smiled at Mary. Suddenly she was no longer invisible.

A waltz with Howard, the exalted beggar.

Thank you for this gift you've made, she said, looking straight at him. His eyes were like a greenish fog, like damp seaweed. The green of stalks that could be parted the better to see the lethargic water beneath. But no, nothing in Howard was lethargic. He was livelier than the living, newer than a newborn, he was ready to bound into the foam, to get drunk on the air, even if it was polluted, to go wild with everything that, in this old, old city, tired of all these charades, still had a child's radiant smile.

In this old land of new evils, Mary, he finally said as he sat down, they learned how to cry for the death of a princess the same way they learned how to forget her after—this new civilization of shaky morals and fleeting tears—and two ten-year-old children could kill a three-year-old child for no reason, with no hatred, can you imagine that, we all thought killing for the fun of it was done only by grown-ups but no, children have always been doing it as well, it's just that now they've switched from insects to people because there's nobody around to tell them what they can or can't do, in this land unpunished crimes are acceptable crimes, we can only judge those who have been caught, and these new evils, Mary, have embedded themselves in the scabs that had already formed over the wounds of the old city, and they will go on doing so. Call no man happy until he is dead.

Feel how light this dance is, and how bright this light that once had been so blinding—now turned by alcohol into the pinpricks of a headache, into bubbles of champagne with their heady, intoxicating fragrance; feel how we are wasting our life on this earth.

Mary listened to him, at once surprised and seduced. Wasting our life on this earth? Was this what she was doing as she slid inexorably toward her death? Was this what happened to people when they got old—the earth working to get rid of them and abandon them almost before they'd died, leaving them as lost as things that people no longer needed? Or were they the ones who were losing their sense of life?

Have we gone astray in this life? Nothing beckons me onward, nothing holds me back. If there were an eraser that could scrub me away . . . said Mary. Howard reached into his satchel and pulled out an artist's eraser. Which part do you want me to erase first? he asked with a smile. Mary considered the question. Not her feet, since she still needed to walk and wander and discover all these new things she'd never even guessed existed. Not her hands, because she still needed to grasp, no matter how maladroitly, the materials of her visions. Not her eyes, because she still wanted to see, and see more of, Howard's face and Cub's face, Cub's body.

Suddenly she knew.

Words, she said, erase my words, because I don't have anything to say that's worth hearing.

With you, I can talk without words.

Tenderly, Howard took her face between his hands, tilted it toward the light. The golden moisture of the air exhaled microscopic droplets on this fragile parchment. Just beneath her skin could be seen the latticework of veins, the bluish network that still traced the trajectory of Mary's life. Howard knew the different phases of Mary, as a precise calendar would those of the moon. He applied the eraser to a mouth that was nothing more than a very pale dividing line, and he set to erasing the words hidden there, all the words of her sadness. Across Mary's blue eyes there flitted a quick fear like the wing of a bird in the night. Then she was calm again as she gave up the words she no longer needed.

Now, said Howard, the only words you have are the happy ones.

When Cub saw Mary walk by, so unseeing that she didn't even notice him, what struck him was the cold surrounding her. Her eyes were white. She was as faded as an old sheet. She had gone out in slippers and was stumbling on the wet sidewalk.

He followed her. Her white eyes made him think of those dolls his mother had given his sisters when they were little. Dolls missing their eyes, their hair, or some of their limbs, corpse-like remnants of that childlike war that kids wrought against their possessions before giving them away to poorer kids. That was what his mother brought back, not long after splitting from his father, when she had gone mad with fury and grief and had unearthed, who knows where, these gifts that made her children shudder.

To make her happy, his little sisters had to sleep next to these empty holes in the middle of the pink faces that never slept, that watched them in the night and haunted their dreams and told them we're the cripples and that's what you'll be, too, by the time life's had its way with you. Growing up far too quickly under their mother's wild eye, they accepted their responsibility to their mother, they knew that any rebuke at all would send her flying to the other side, that she considered those dolls a way of telling them that she could take care of them, that she didn't need a man or any official papers, that her fear of the police didn't keep her from caring for her family even if the lightest knock at the door left her shaking like a little dog so that one of the children, standing on a chair to look through the peephole, would have to confirm that it wasn't the police.

Mary was walking like the maimed, unseeing dolls of his nightmares. He followed her as if he were responsible for her; when she skidded in her slippers a sharp cry escaped her lips. Her hair was as unkempt as straw stalks in the wind. Nobody stopped her, people moved away from her rather than touch her, but they could hear the spongy squeak of her slippers, a delicate sound like porcelain, and they let her stumble toward nothingness.

Her footsteps seemed light, so light, as if she was walking on a cushion of air, on a cushion of laughter.

Her thoughts were still filled by Howard. The flecks of gold in the air around her, that wild sun—like nothing she'd ever seen in November—that the bundled-up passersby seemed not to notice. On the contrary, they watched her, astonished, as she walked without a coat. The way the light was flowing over her hands reminded her that when she was a teenager she had sweetened her tea with honey. She'd taken an overflowing spoonful from the honey pot and let it drip in a long, thin thread into the weak tea. Then her lips had eagerly closed around the rest of the honey still on the spoon, a paste that sealed her mouth shut.

This light is like honey on her lips: it flows and sticks at the same time.

Mary began to laugh. She was talking aimlessly and

not a single sound was escaping her lips, she was talking to a space in the air that Cub thought he could maybe make out, she was waving her hands, but he couldn't tell who she was responding to; the boy furrowed his brows, worried. Should he ignore her? Act like he didn't know her, like she was just an elderly neighbor who didn't matter? He still wasn't sure whether it was chance or something more intentional that had brought him to Portobello Road that day. But in any case there he was. Life, their meetings, the road, his thoughts. Everything disappeared in its own time, at its own speed, but everything disappeared. Mary, too, had entered an intermediary space; soon, he knew, she would no longer be there.

He kept on following her with an inexplicable lump in his throat.

Angels. Our angels. Who are they? How do they come to us?

A light turning itself off, a door opening in winter, the shadows of branches crisscrossing on a wall despite there being no tree. If people believe in ghosts, and in signs, then why not in angels? And, on the flimsiest of pretexts, knowing that they're not fooling anyone, least of all themselves, they decide to follow them anyway.

Isn't that what people have always wanted to do?

Follow in an angel's footsteps?

That's not the hardest thing, Mary thought. The hardest thing is to do what it says.

What is it saying?

It's not the impetus of a blue sky that carries us but far less clement weather, with drizzle and fog. Following an angel's footsteps means trudging through the despair it catches with its magnetic feet. It means having one's only food be the bitterness that flows from its lips. Do you really believe we eat toast slathered with honey? Even if we do have sweet breath that gives all that we touch the freshest of flavors. What use is it to be an angel if we can't make these silent paths welcoming? But our passage through the world is a harbinger of death. Do not forget that if you see an angel, your days are numbered.

Mary came back home, filled with light. Cub had followed her hesitantly. He had the impression that she was slipping beyond all hope, that little was left of the energy that had filled her body, and that, if he wasn't there, nothing would hold on to it. As with his mother, as with his sisters and his brother, Cub had the impression he was holding Mary's life in his hands.

Ever since they had returned, Mary had barely spoken. But she looked at him with so much delight in her eyes that he was worried. He didn't understand this unfounded joy. She was trembling and smiling like a young girl. She looked at herself in the mirror and primped her hair like a diva. Cub felt lost. Who was she talking to? What had brought about this abrupt transformation?

Warmth, that was what mattered, he needed to make sure this reassuring, calm woman with a smooth forehead and a silent mouth stayed warm.

She had forgotten to eat. It was he who cooked and fed her like a child while she went on smiling so absentmindedly that it scared him.

She said only one sentence: "You're my angel." Then she choked, as if talking hurt her, although it was in fact a laugh caught in her throat.

Mary felt young, younger than she'd ever been. Howard had given her back her youth. She felt prettier than Mary Rose: not only was she not a virgin, but she was also sensual and desirable. She undid the straps of an imaginary dress, which wasn't a flowery dress for a ball but a tight raw-silk dress from which her bare breasts peeked out like the orbs she had never had.

She looked adoringly at Cub, forgetting that she was in love with Howard (maybe they were one and the same). Her head was filled with a violet vertigo and her body with a slow waltz. Old age no longer had any hold on her.

She turned on the radio, and the lyrics that surged forth were promises to take her by the hand and walk her through London, to show her something that would change her mind. She smiled in recognition: it was a Ralph McTell song, Howard's song.

She held her hand out to Cub. Despite his uncertainty he took it. She pulled him into a dance, unwittingly breaking both their hearts.

Through the window, he could see the clear outline of an airplane bisecting the sky. The passengers were in another world, between heaven and earth, between two spaces, suspended between life and the possibility of death. Did they know what would become of them between taking off and landing? The world had changed in the wake of those two fallen towers. He and Mary, too, were suspended between opposing possibilities.

This house was an airplane that held them in this uneasy balance. They shouldn't leave it: they'd immediately fall into the prisonlike horror that was the real world, with its prison bars of prohibitions and its explosives.

And why would there be so many prohibitions? Mary wondered, dancing, dancing. She felt younger and younger. Howard watched her from the ceiling with a knowing smile. Go on, Mary, he said, don't be afraid to live. None of us has lived. Fear has imprisoned us all. And for what?

We're passengers in a plane that might—or might not—crash. And between those two possibilities there's the vast range of life.

In her arms, she felt Cub's trembling body. She sensed, without understanding, the odor of the drugs in him that were immobilizing him. As if, at the same time, he both understood nothing and understood everything with a clarity so vivid that it paralyzed him.

Cub danced with her, feeling a deep shame. He saw a woman who wanted to be happy at all costs at the very end of her life, and he alone was able to offer her this happiness, even if his entire body rebelled against the very thought.

Night seeped into their waltz. The earth stopped momentarily, as if there were impossible facts to consider. Mary's euphoria, which was outside time itself, was clear to Cub, who forgot who they were and only felt this sensation of a strange death-stricken youth, who forgot that this flesh was practically nonexistent, and who only saw the light filtering through her skin, and they spun until all Cub had in his hands was a glass figure at the heart of which burned a flame that he had never in his short life seen before.

Late in the night, exhausted, they climbed up to the bedroom beneath Howard's wings. The angel guided Mary, who guided Cub. She had uttered only a few words the whole night. Her eyes, however, had never been so communicative, nor her hands so effusive. And hers weren't the faded eyes and the worn-out hands of the old woman whose house and bed he had been sleeping in all this time. In the decrepit house, he saw Mary undergoing a rebirth and the sight stirred up an unexpected tumult within him.

In the bedroom, she pointed to the hole in the ceiling and held her finger to her lips, her eyes sparkling. She could hear Howard's shivering laugh (accompanied by the smell of methane: maybe it was some discreet gas?). Cub looked at the hole, then at Mary. He was stupefied to see her undoing the belt of her dress, pulling down its zipper, and letting it fall to the floor. Feeling nauseated, he shut his eyes.

When Mary's hands touched his face, he forced his eyes open again. Mary made him look at her. Her smile hinted that beyond the thin, angular body with blue creases, the flattened breasts where light pink nipples were visible, the flabby belly that no longer covered a soft layer of fat but rather showed organs nearing failure, the thighs streaked by veins, the face carved by wrinkles but which had retained its triangular shape and the fluidity of her gaze, the thinning hair, beyond this wholesale erosion of every attractive feature, of every appealing trait, of every charm, there was another presence: the gleaming illusion of a woman. She still existed, she had never left. She was visible now, casting aside all the ravages of time. She waved her fingers momentarily freed from their arthritis and shaped her own flesh to give it forms that had long since gone. She became a sculptor again: her medium now was herself.

Why hadn't she been able to mold herself until now? he wondered with a devastated heart. Why had she been forbidden from living?

As he sank into Mary's gaze and smile, Cub stopped

seeing her as she had been and saw her as she was revealing herself to be. He forgot everything. She ran her fingers over his face and his neck, she took off his jumper and his cap, and gently undressed him, both like a child and like a man. The feeling of this fragile skin filled Cub with astonishment, because it was as beautiful as a nighttime breeze over his hot forehead. He let himself relax.

Now, there was nothing left in Cub but the thought of Mary, this old dream of Mary Rose that Howard had instilled from the hole in the ceiling, and which Mary intensified with the force of her own desire. Angels are capable of miracles, she said to herself, and we're angels, we can become angels, and so great was her conviction that, as the earth momentarily stopped, she literally transformed in front of Cub's eyes, became pink and white, became dark blond and turquoise blue, became an embracing lover, thrumming with life.

She lay Cub on her bed, relishing the beauty of this unmoving body, of these heavy-lidded eyes, and, nude as well, she taught him things that he had not yet experienced and that she had thought she'd never known. She was no longer seventy-five years old, nor was he thirteen. Even as the world looked away, nothing marred the beauty of her outstretched body, no gaze defiled her.

Cub's body reacted while his spirit was seized by a surge of pleasure. He didn't think of anyone. Not his mother, not his sisters, not his friends. What happened seemed no more impossible than the fact that he had been standing in front of the house that day when she was walking out. Everything had brought them here, to this moment beyond time and beyond limits.

Mary kneeled, her legs on each side of Cub. Her body exuded an aroma of old waxed marble, but also of greenery, of rosemary and thyme. On the inside of her thigh there was a teardrop, a pearl, a single silvery drop. She lowered herself slowly upon Cub's stiff member, overjoyed that he was still watching her, that he hadn't shut his eyes. She looked up and saw Howard's eye peering through the hole. All three of them were united here, united like Mary's interlocked statuettes, like the new lovers of that new era had been when they decided to rebuild the city. Her hands caressed Cub's too-soft skin, her fingers paused momentarily on the odd battle scars, then touched his moist lips. She leaned forward and pressed her lips to his, tasting their spongy firmness, then slipped down to his small, flat torso, wholly male with its purple tips pointing upward in the darkness. She felt herself becoming the white angel that would absorb Cub and feed on his flesh, his energy, his life.

Their climax was simultaneous, a moment of extraordinary violence.

Did anyone see them?

Did someone watch them through the window? The two of them, there, sleeping intertwined like an old couple. Easily overcoming in their blissful ignorance the breach generally considered impossible, the mysterious finality, the last of all taboos. The ultimate prohibition for the living because, for the dead, there were none.

This love was not visible to anyone, did not renounce anything, did not elude any possibility, thought Mary. I'd love my son just the same way I'd love a man just the same way I'd love a father. A thousand ways and all of them the same.

Even so, Mary, tossing and turning in her sleep, didn't want to wake up because all her certainties would collapse in front of the open eye. She saw what was irrevocable. She clenched her fists around her sleep, her arms around Cub. Morning would only bring ruin, and the despair of a light too raw to let anyone believe in angels and miracles.

All that would remain of her would be the short, trampled grass she had always been. An entire city had gone over her body. An entire city had entered her body. Its weight, its matter, its texture, its place beneath a blue or gray or black sky. Steel, concrete, brick, stone, terracotta, granite, quartz—strata built up over millions of years that she thought she could feel in her hands, supple or rough, burning or porous, she had experienced it all, she had explored the labyrinths of the past, she had been part of the flesh of this land, nothing could separate her from it.

She would have liked to give Cub another world that they could have watched being born at his birth, a world they could have lived in together. A world built out of something other than monoliths of steel, Leviathans of iron, layers of gas.

Her only chance at love was Cub. The round, swelling love of a glorious monster.

To lose him . . . She opened her eyes and forced herself to look those words straight on. She thought she could see a tear starting at the bottom of her torso, between her thighs. She propped herself up on her knees and looked at his face. She felt humble, prayerful. Nothing mattered now. She waited for the bit of daylight that would glide over his eyelids and eyelashes, that would awaken him. His sullen mouth would let out a painful groan as he woke up and his young body would stretch out its limbs even as it had yet to understand the extent of its joy and its beauty.

Lose him? No, Mary swore, keeping her gaze fixed on him. I'd die before I lost him. I'd kill before I lost him.

A sliver of awareness within her knew the risk she was taking. The social workers were there, ready to ambush her. If she didn't put up a fight, they would seize her and throw her in one of those prisonlike places where the dead, having no fight left in them, went to die. Where each one ended up alone with their crumpled-up memories, even though they were never really alone. Where each one was trapped in a hostile world. The old people looked like aliens, Mary thought, barricaded in their loneliness and their foreignness. They were stripped of all humanity by rigid regulations, revolting food, surveillance, suspicion, sometimes even violence. They no longer had a right to intimacy, no longer had a right to anything, they had to do their business under the cold glare of someone else, pull down their underwear while looking at their feet, let themselves be washed like hideous babies. And there they stayed, imbuing the air, layer upon layer, with their stench, their thoughts, their distress.

In this way the souls of old people were reduced to larvae haunting the mortal seasons until, one terribly cold or horribly hot day, their life finally agreed to loosen its hold and let them sleep, sleep for good in the soft, weak bed of their skin.

In this way the old people went, if they didn't fight.

I won't go, Mary thought. I'll fight. I'd rather die first. And I'd rather kill first. She clenched her arms around her sleep and her fists around Cub.

Cub woke up and looked at her. She was sure his gaze was loving. Maybe she wasn't wrong.

Cub walked in the snow, stomping it here and there into mud beneath his trainers, sometimes floating above it without leaving a trace. A bus dipped into a lake of half-melted snow, splattering him with liquefied ice. He stepped to the side, but too late. A few people nearby sniggered, despite their frozen faces. The sky was so low it could almost be touched. Cub didn't reply with curses or a raised fist as he once would have; he was following a narrow path, living enchanted days, he was following the siren songs of seraphim toward a light so near it could almost be touched.

From a café there wafted the aromas of warm drinks and melting butter; a small newspaper seller smiled at him under her red beret, standing behind a barricade of nude women on glossy paper. He heard the squishing of his own feet and the screech of car and bus axles, and he saw the burst of red that was the young girl's beret. He started running and his footsteps pounded a melody in his head.

It was a rhythm he knew well, although he had no idea where it had come from. Tip tatap tatap tip. Skater skirts, not from his time so much as from his mother's time, when she was young and she rubbed cream on her smooth, perfectly oval face and painted her nails garnet to go out to the clubs and, when she came back late at night, she would kiss them, and her stilettos, on the floor, click-clacked in a familiar way, yes, this was his mother's rhythm, tap tippy tap. These days, girls only ever wore trousers or miniskirts that clung to their bottoms and crop tops that were tight around their breasts, and this seemed cute and sexy to him, of course, but what he was hearing in his head made him think of a skirt made from thick, smooth fabric, lined with silk, swirling around a woman's calves, a red beret on her head.

Tip tatap tatap tip.

Running, racing, rushing into the foamy snow that crackled softly, dusting Cub's hair with icing sugar as if he were a succulent pastry. For a few seconds, just a few seconds, the city was as white and light as a silk-lined skirt, it skated on high heels and the sun reflected in the crystals of snow poured warm gold into his eyes through the threads of flitting cloth, the living cloth of the city, scarf, bus, cars, magazines, phone booths, tip tap tippy tap tip.

Cub had never realized that he could love this city, find it both unnerving and alluring. Nothing was as it had been before, everything had changed since meeting Mary on Portobello Road. Ever since the night before, each of his steps had felt padded. The road had been made of clouds rather than snow. Ever since the night before, all the women had been within reach.

He didn't understand himself, he didn't know what had happened the night before. Something—or maybe somebody—had entered him. His spirit refused to dwell on it for too long: he knew he would have to make sense of it at some point. Of what? I smoked too much, I slept and dreamed, he thought, but deep down a warmth made it clear that there had only been a dance and then sleep.

Mary had been changed, transformed, made beautiful. The illusion of wings spreading out. A strange, wondrous dance. He shook his head to stop thinking about it. (An old hag, she's just an old hag—no, not at all: she's Mary.)

Forgetting the lights of Portobello Road and its vicinity and making his way into the hustle and bustle of Brixton, Cub went from one world to another. He still had the warmth of desire in his core and eyes filled with beating wings, but he was coming back, little by little, to the real world he'd known before Mary, the color of everybody's face here was familiar, as were their quick smiles and sly looks, the sounds and smells reaching out to bring him back to reality.

Graffiti blazed on the walls. Boys and girls were walking with a nonchalance that felt dangerous. Jobless men tried to disappear into the sidewalks. The women's jaws were clenched. He saw the barricaded, boarded-up windows, the corners where he could buy his choice of drugs, guns or girls. These were fortresses that the police, in their powerlessness, avoided. Brixton thrived on this toxic trade, which threatened the entire city. The deeper anyone went down these alleys, the clearer it became that a rigidly structured guerrilla organization was biding its time. He knew the landmarks that divided the territories. He knew which neighborhoods he shouldn't wander into, because the other gangs wouldn't do him any favors. He knew which shirt colors and which symbols meant danger and violence. He knew where a new coat of paint covered huge splatters of blood and brain matter.

A few eyes met Cub's. Some he recognized, and some recognized him. Rather than the gestures they usually made, he saw hesitation, glances slipping out of reach.

Someone turned away and sniggered. This didn't bother him. Teenagers trying to act like adults, in gaudy clothes and gold-plated bling, shrugged as they saw him, as if to warn him that he was headed down a dangerous path, a path of no return, if he didn't return to their ranks straight-away. A shrug of their shoulders, an elegant "tsk," a brief wave to say, there are preordained paths you should follow, and others you should avoid like the plague: you need to pick a side.

Cub had already gone too far beyond his old life and his old ways to contemplate how he could return. And he wasn't so sure he even wanted to. He was more intrigued by the freedom that Portobello Road had granted him, a freedom that may have been cold and strange, but was still seductive, as if he had grown up before his time and had got a taste of the powers that adults had, of the powers that even adults did not have.

He had the impression that the light was absorbed by particular neighborhoods while others were plunged into semidarkness. Brixton had developed like so many other neighborhoods that had once been scorned by the city, with trendy shops and restaurants and bars, but his heart still belonged to those shadows from which he had emerged. These areas were designed to keep their hold on humanity. So many doors, so many mouths opening up to swallow up people. They would always swallow up the unwary Jonahs who wandered in. And the taller the build-ings rose, the deeper men sank in their vertigo.

In the building where his mother lived, the walls weren't even visible anymore. In the entrance hall, the reek of joints weighed down the air of this glebe. The unpainted walls exuded damp and, in the darkest nooks, mushrooms. (One morning, in their flat, his mother had burst out laughing when she saw the gray living-room carpet covered in mushrooms that had sprouted overnight.) In Cub's building, everyone blindly groped their way forward just to live. Some ended up walking straight out open windows.

As he came closer, Cub felt no shiver of sentimentality. He knew this place where he had been born by heart. He felt no shame at having lived there, just as he had felt no shame at leaving it. Here, there was no strange attachment nor indulgent nostalgia. He didn't dress up his memories in finery. He set them somewhere so they would have no further hold.

He rang the doorbell. He heard shouts and barking. The door opened and once again there was the smell of something burning, just like the other day, as if he'd been living the same day forever. His little sister, Sondra, looked at him, her face wet with tears. She was holding a shirt with holes in it. Their mother appeared, glanced at Cub distractedly, pulled the shirt out of the little girl's hands and threw it in the bin. She started shaking her so hard her teeth chattered. "I've just bought this shirt for you and you've managed to burn it!" A dog yipped excitedly. Jasmine came out of her bedroom, her face caked in makeup. "You look like a slut! Yes, a slut! A slut!" Wanda yelled. Jasmine, wearing a yellow crop top that didn't even try to hide her heavy breasts, stretchy jeans that molded her bottom and stilettos that were more like stilts, shrugged and shook her hair, which now came down to her lower back. Her teeth gleamed brightly in her lipsticked mouth. Cub could tell that she was trying to piss off their mother.

She shoved Cub aside as she stomped out of the flat.

On her face was a slight smirk, as if she wasn't bothered one bit by Wanda's hysteria. She started making her way down the stairs rather than bother to wait for the elevator, and Cub suddenly heard it, that familiar tippy tap tippy tap. It had been passed down to a new generation. It was this willowy yet padded, firm yet flowing body that now held him in place. The locks of hair bounced gently, with the exact same rhythm, on her plump buttocks. Cub shut his eyes and let his mind be carried away by that mysterious pattern. It didn't matter if the past was burning: the rhythm would go on bouncing happily from one generation to the next, and it would never be lost.

He turned back to his mother. She was standing rigidly straight with her fists clenched and her eyes filled with tears. The last time he had seen her, she had smiled at the gift of a handbag. He sensed that she didn't have any money left at all and that she didn't know how she'd make it to the end of the month. How she'd keep them all alive. Her misery was so clearly etched in this empty gaze. He pulled a twenty-pound note that he'd taken from Mary out of his pocket and held it out to her. She grabbed the note with a sort of fury. Then she sighed and went to sit down in her usual chair. He followed her.

"Where'd you get this money from?" she asked. "I don't want you getting mixed up with gangs. The Brixton cops already arrested some boys this week. They were all the way from eleven years old to sixteen. Tell me the truth. Where'd you get this from?"

He didn't answer, and she kept going. She wrung her hands, bit her lips, tapped her bare feet—she hadn't worn high heels in ages. Cub noted each of her thoughts, each of her feelings. He cursed himself for not being older, so he could help them all out. He knelt down, took her feet in his hands and began massaging them.

"Mum, I'll take care of you and everyone else. Don't worry."

"You haven't got a job. How are you going to get money? I'm the one who has to take care of you, Cub. You should go back to school, I know you haven't been going, the teachers called and told me."

Because he had no excuses, Cub tried to offer some semblance of the truth.

"There's an old lady on Portobello Road who's taken me in. I've been doing work on her house, I'm running errands for her and she's been paying me. I'll bring you the money each week."

"What's her name?"

"Mary. Mary Grimes."

As he said it, Cub realized he had made a mistake. But it was too late. And besides, she had every right to know. His mother's eyes darkened.

"And why does she want you living with her? You can do your work without living in her moldy house!"

"Mum . . . How do you know her house has mold?"

"I know what it must be like, what she must look like, your old woman with her house on Portobello Road . . . Everything must be falling apart, and even then she's going to feel superior to you because she's paying you!"

He sighed. There was no way he could possibly explain Mary Grimes to her. He could feel the jealousy that was making her shake.

"Cub . . . She's an old white woman . . . she's using you. You don't need to do that to live . . . I want you to go back to school. I promise you I'll manage."

Of course he knew she would. Tap tap tippy tippy tap . . . His mother had had rhythms that Mary would never know.

"Mum . . ."

He didn't know what to say. He kissed her hands one by one, and Wanda's eyes filled with a sort of stupid happiness. He knew that, when he left, she would ask herself all the same questions any mother should ask. She looked at him but could not understand; she only sensed just how much he had changed, no, not changed, transformed, completely from the inside out. She was slowly losing Cub, her Cub, the child she'd always loved, always hoped for, the one she trusted when she stonewalled the other children, because some witch had captured him. She held his face in her hands.

"Stay here, don't go back there. I'll pull myself together, I'll find another job and sort everything out. Stay, I need you here."

He shook his head, knowing he couldn't come back. It was too late for that. "We'll figure it out, don't worry," she said, wearily. "Don't go back there, Cub."

He kissed her forehead and saw the fear hidden in her eyes. It was because of Cub. She was scared for him—or maybe of him. She clung to him and refused to let go. Cub had to extricate himself as gently as he could.

"Watch Jasmine," he said. "She's going to get into trouble."

"She already has," his mother said, almost indifferently.

Cub noticed that there wasn't a television in the living room anymore. Almost no furniture. The paint was peeling off the walls. A draft was blowing in through a broken fanlight. He had the feeling that their flat was soon going to look just like the house on Portobello Road, and that worms would start falling from the ceiling. Maybe they'd all been caught in a gust of dilapidation that would spare none of them?

"I can't do anything to manage Jasmine," she said. "Not by myself I can't. I know how she'll end up, with a bun in the oven and no baby daddy to be found. Just like me. Just like me."

"Mum . . ."

"Don't say anything, Cub. It's not worth it. I'll have to buy clothes at Oxfam soon. And I'll get a summons in the post."

His eyes shifted to the window. He stopped there. He pressed his body against it, filled with both desire and terror.

"Mum, I swear to you this old lady's going to help us. She's going to die soon, she doesn't have anybody, maybe she'll leave me her house! Do you hear me? A house on Portobello Road! We could all live there easy. Just wait, hang in there. I know what I'm doing."

Cub was saying anything he could to distract his mother from the temptation of the window.

He tried not to think of Mary's eyes, but pushing her out of his mind felt like a betrayal.

"I don't understand what that woman wants from you. You know they have the police after people who have done less?"

"Less than what?"

"What does she want from you?"

He didn't reply.

I don't know, Cub thought to himself. I don't know what

she wants from me and what I want from her. It's all a haze in my head. That first day, standing in front of her house, with the window that wouldn't shut, I was smoking and thinking it would be so easy to sneak in that way, to see what was inside. I wouldn't have done it. I wouldn't have broken in, even if I was thinking about it. Then she came out, I must have thought she was ugly, old ladies are always a nightmare to look at, but she wasn't like the others. She seemed transparent. Like she was made of fog, smoke, a wisp of cloud. And her eyes, so blue in the middle of that white. The way she held my hand. I didn't understand it at all. She didn't disgust me.

She still didn't disgust him. Nor did her house, which must have struck him as horrifying. He had crossed a boundary. He was in London, but it wasn't the same city anymore. I've a feeling we're not in Kansas anymore, he whispered, smiling a bit. Deep down, he felt like Dorothy, carried by a tornado to another world, another dimension, where he wasn't Cub and where Mary was . . . something else. How could he have, if not . . .

He shook his head violently to keep himself from thinking about that night. The night of gray cats and soft, downy flesh slipping between cold sheets under the eye of a corpse.

As he left the flat, and his mother, and Brixton, with a slow tread, he couldn't shake the feeling of a door closing behind him. Somehow, the familiar words of Bob Marley came to mind: *My feet is my only carriage, so I've got to push on through.*

He remembered. He stepped over a disgusting puddle at the base of a building. He looked down and saw nothing reflected back.

Go, go, go, said the bird: human kind
Cannot bear very much reality.
Time past and time future
What might have been and what has been
Point to one end, which is always present.

   —T. S. ELIOT, *Four Quartets: Burnt Norton*

He was sure of it now. His mind had resisted the possibility as far as it could, but now he had to concede the truth about himself.

That other evening, leaving his mother's place, he had gone to King's Cross St Pancras to see his friends. He heard the furious roars and felt the vibrations of the trains deep within his belly. A sort of icy dread or premonition had kept him from going in. The people were coming in and out of the station in a long, unchanging flood. Hurried and frozen at the same time, all of them alike, their gazes identical. The flow of faces had erased all individuality, the constant swing of hands and feet had blurred them all into uniformity. Cub walked against the flow, against its will. He felt the oncoming flow of the human flood as if it were trying to push him backward. He had wanted to let himself be carried away. The station doors seemed to open wide to seize him. He knew this place so well, but in this moment he didn't feel like he was returning; it seemed to want to shut him out, he was at the mercy of a fate that refused to let him go so long as he didn't remember everything.

He had the impression that the train station's medieval sculptures had multiplied: dragons with crocodiles' bodies, griffins with eagles' wings, gargoyles with vultures' necks. Beneath the arches, vast and empty spaces awaited his gaze, awaited his scrutiny of their shadows. Gothic and Victorian, the two neighboring stations, King's Cross and St Pancras, false twins, extended outward, the one within the other, chased one another, bit their own tails. There were so many details to examine, like these tiny windows that a blue light would pass through at a specific hour of the day and which otherwise were invisible, doors that closed off long-untouched attics. All this created a black hole of strangeness. To look up would mean losing all sense of what was straight ahead.

He made his way toward the bridge that some people called "the suicide bridge." Someone had told Cub that the most suicides in London happened there—more even than in the Thames. He sniffed the air. He could smell their fear, their despair and their exaltation at the moment of jumping off. Could you step off this bridge? he wondered. He'd also heard that dying under a train was the least painful way to go. He couldn't understand that. He couldn't imagine a more painful way of killing himself, other than by fire. Someone in the gang had bragged about having a good shag one night on this bridge, in the hot steam blasted from the trains, the smell of sulfur and soot, under a steel vault. "I'd never come so hard!" he said, and they'd all laughed. But he'd added that, when they'd finished, the girl's white dress had ended up covered in black specks, as if the hand of death had touched it. Today, Cub, on the bridge, wondered whether he would come just as hard here, in the darkness, the wind, the smoke, the metal—a stern, narrow world, like a planet that wasn't Earth, inhabited by stone and steel beings—or whether the hand of death would touch him.

Even if he turned this hand down, he knew that she would call him with a distant voice, she wouldn't let him run away, she wanted him, she lusted for him, she held him, she was the angel come to find him and throw him from the bridge and he had to let her guide and carry him, lead him like a lamb to the slaughter, he could cry, sniffle, sob, but nothing would make a difference. It was decided. The gargoyles and the dragons would accompany him, their voices sharp, but without mockery, they would know that there were places marked by this seal and that some ventured here, risking their lives—or their deaths.

It was at this moment that he made the connection. Here, at this exact instant that he'd climbed up the bridge.

Could he be up here and down there at the same time? In this no-man's-land, so far outside his limits, he could take that risk, he could become as primordial as an amoeba and forget his body, his sad eyes, his presumably dreamless days. And pull on the thread that would bring him back to himself. Was it possible that he'd never even existed?

On the bridge of the damned, he understood that he had meant to rob the old woman. It was that simple: he was a thief. If she'd fought back, he might have even killed her without much thought. Only pure chance had kept him from committing murder. Then she'd looked at him with her odd eyes, a dizzying upwelling of love, and that desire had gone out from within her, leaving behind something else, a boy who was no longer a child, not yet a man. On the bridge of final moments, he told himself he didn't need to be ashamed. There were far stranger, uglier things in this world, in Brixton's buildings where fathers fucked their daughters and grandparents their dogs. And gang rapes in basements so far underground that, as in outer space, nobody heard the screams. Gang rapes he might have taken part in, high on crack despite his mother's fury, barely seeing the contorted face and the bottom of the giant, gaping mouth out of which came piggish squeals, and everything he saw was one dripping crack or another, oily and reddened by too much friction before finally dripping with blood, it was utterly inhuman, it was simply a place to stick his dick in, just like all the others, there hadn't been anything more to it, anything worth thinking about.

Around him, he didn't see a place but a world that he filled with his sperm. An old land that he was transforming with his blood, his energy, his vigor. "I'd fuck an old land to bring it back to life," he whispered. "I'll take the world with all my come." He was seized by a despair so ancient it seemed to have been the residue of this very space, a despair encompassing his mother, his cousins, his neighborhood, a despair at this dissolution of entities that altered small parts of the world and never the whole, just the parts that bent toward violence. A despair that engulfed him in a revelation of his uselessness, of how wholly unexceptional his absence would be. Like a barely visible shooting star, the question crossed his heart: What difference would I have made?

His hands gripped the barrier and he wondered if he had the courage. He stood up on his tiptoes. What if? What if? A train neared, venting a thick, black violence. What if? The noise ran through the rails, shook the bridge and Cub too. What if? The heat seeped through his pores, sank into his entire body like so many needles. What if?

Slowly, Cub raised his foot and set it on the lowest crossbar of the barrier.

"Hey, wog, need some help?" a voice asked.

His foot came back down on the bridge and he saw six men walking his way. They were fat, swollen, red-blooded, thoroughly drunk. Their cheeks were flushed. Each had his own boozy swagger. Their shaven heads set off hundreds of alarm bells. The silver necklaces with crucifixes or swastikas hanging off them. Their fingers encased in knuckle-dusters. The tattoos, the studs, the boots.

Cub gave them a stupid smile and held up his hands, palms facing the men to show that he wasn't dangerous. They smiled, too, baring their rotting teeth to show that they were.

Nobody was near. Nobody would be near. The guys had a sixth sense that steered them clear of trouble. They closed in on him. A warmth snaked its way down his legs and he realized, in shock, that it was piss. He hadn't realized just how scared he was.

He knew he was going to die.

They reeked of sweat, beer-soured breath, cigarettes and unwashed clothes. And their skin, most of all, their white skin mottled with red, streaked with bloody scratches, had a recognizably, horribly animalistic smell. The odor bound him where he was before their faces had even entered his field of vision. This stench of hordes ready to turn violent, leeching off his fear as if it were a drug, this scent petrified and paralyzed him, it made him reel as the hands reached out to him.

Just as they were about to touch him, he found his strength. He bolted in the other direction.

Bile rose up in his throat and reached his teeth. It

dripped out as he ran. And maybe something else, something that dissipated when it was clear that there was no use hanging on to the improbable ballast of a fleeing body.

Fear, just as much as the hatred that radiated from their bodies, urged him onward. That was what had scared him most. A chemical stench. The odor of this hate had frozen him for a moment as with those animals who sprayed their prey with a paralyzing agent. But the same primal instinct of panic had enabled him to escape.

He was so unaccustomed to this sensation of flight, this burst of untrammeled strength. He had been on the other side; like them he had tasted the flavor of fear. Now he knew he only had a small chance left—which was to flee.

They weren't human. Nor were they animals. They were relics.

Cub reached the bottom of the bridge. The train went by. He was overcome by the noise, the gusts of hot air as it kept going. He didn't feel anything anymore as the train obliterated its shadow.

Rows of dragons and griffins and odd animals made out of stone and dust and incisions stretched as far as he could see. It was cold, very cold, either within himself or outside. He couldn't be sure. In his mind, the fantastical array of beasts watched him with their bare eyes. Dragons, griffins, phoenixes—although he barely knew those names. He saw, with absolute clarity, that his final vision was all around him. Then this thought, too, disappeared, and all he could remember was that hatred.

He ran. With all his strength. With all the energy his small body, used to folding up or contorting or dancing or being torn, could muster. His steps took him instinctively toward Portobello Road, toward Mary, toward this chance encounter that was now his lodestone. It was only a potential refuge. (Brixton was too far away, getting back there would be impossible.) He ran there. He flew there. (His heart didn't remind him that Portobello Road was too far away, that Portobello Road was now in the pliable world of Oz.)

The possibility of love that he'd glimpsed in the light of Mary's face when he'd seen her for the first time. That possibility alone spoke to him. Filled him, entered him through every pore and every opening and every brutal wound. Flooded him, flushed out all the blood he would lose all too soon. This long race through London. So light on his dancer's feet that he bounded down so many kilometers without feeling tired, and yet they kept on following him, they hadn't given up, they climbed onward like giants, as if they owned the earth, and that was how they saw things, free for the taking, as was their right, and each step they took as they ran was a claim on a bit more land, they swallowed up kilometers of pavement, swelling their unrelenting desire like a wildfire, while for Cub, each step he took was toward abandonment and defeat, toward the moment when he would stop and turn and look at them, knowing that this would be his last retrenchment, his last confrontation before experiencing his death. And it would be a respite.

The roads unfurled. The black facades oiled by rain, the splotches of the past, the surges of the future, the corners he thought he knew but which now presented an unfamiliar face, the edges, the lines, the profiles of the entire city, this city he thought had been his own, that he'd thought was manifold, colorful and open, it all closed up like a fist as he raced through. Nothing held him back now; it was because there would be nothing left at the end.

He didn't know how he got to Portobello Road; Mary's house gleamed under a heavy sky as distant as a light-house, the only one strong enough to keep him going despite the pain in his muscles, despite his heart being ready to burst out of his chest. He was accompanied by the skinheads' footfalls as they pursued him, filled with enough booze and drugs and hate to not let go, to keep up with him, being, like him, marathoners without knowing it, who would never see a brick wall that could hold them back. Cub was the prey. They were the hunters. They would not let go.

When he came to Portobello Road, a wild, furious hope invaded him: the idea that he might have enough time to knock and enter Mary's house and shut the door behind him. Mary would protect him. Mary alone. But the foot-steps were too close. If he turned around, he would meet their heavy breath. He banged his fists against the door. He didn't know why he had come back here, where noth-ing but the smile of an old woman awaited him. He kept on knocking and knocking with all his strength.

He didn't have time to prepare himself for the dark-ness. They were already around him, shouting at him, sniggering, driving death into his belly like sperm into a womb. His fragility touched their hearts, but not as much as the flower of violence now blossoming in their torsos and their crotches did. They were on home turf: their vic-tim had no hope of any help. Nobody would open their door to the sound of his screams.

Without warning, an iron-encased fist slammed into Cub's nose. Then came other blows in other places, a prolonged battery that made him wish for the ultimate end. He struggled at first not to scream, but when a boot plowed into his stomach, he howled.

It was that sound that opened up the gap that could never be closed again; the words that followed wrenched open new waterways, bloodways, and he, the prey, accepted, as every prey did, the fact of his weakness and his predators' strength, bowing before them, abandoning in submission his right to life and to things. He was on the ground, held down by hands that had no sympathy for him, that were only there to make him suffer, nothing else, all they saw in him was his color: his black betrayed him. Finally, when he saw the blade unfurling from one of his assailants' fists, he smiled.

This smile unnerved the skinheads. The one who had raised the knife didn't bring it down immediately. He held it in the air, his gaze boring into Cub's, tracking the expressions playing out there, following their slow, lucid progression, each shift a realization, each second filled to the brim with radiant truth. Nothing outside weighed him down. The man contemplated the eyes of his victim, perhaps there was a tiny tremor of compassion from deep within the arid landscape of his soul, maybe he thought that this boy bore some small resemblance to his little brother, aside from his skin, and his hair, and his lips, and his nostrils, but soon enough this thought gave way to another, more ritualistic one, the ugliness of this color, this hair, these lips, these nostrils, and so he sank the sharp blade into Cub's belly.

His life took its time. It let itself be seized and tasted, it escaped and left behind all its flavors. Cub relived the taste of burgers, hot fries, cold milkshakes, even Wanda's burnt steaks. Cub tasted the smallest particle of life in his mouth, the bright redness of his gums, the springiness of his tongue, the thickness of his saliva, the whiteness of his teeth. His tongue was dry and he knew that there wouldn't be any more saliva to assuage it.

Then he smelled the scent of corporeal release, of a body that had given up, that had lost the game, as its fluids escaped one by one, sweat soaking his T-shirt like dry wine, strong, undeniably masculine and *his*, and his cargo pants sticky and disgusting. All this contrasted with the calmness in his mouth. Only the odors kept on speaking, pleading, hurting. The last human conversation that could be had when almost nothing human remained, or rather when everything that remained was too human, and the man was merely body, the body was merely animal, the animal was merely rot.

His eyes no longer saw anything, not even the shock of the skinhead hypnotized by their light, but merely disparate colors that came together and then apart without any rhyme or reason, with only some small measure of consolation—it was so rare that the sky over London was ever that blue, verging on obsidian black, and he was so happy to see the pinpricks of stars, and the silvery wing of a vulture sweeping across that blue, its beak awaiting his flesh, so happy not to feel any fear. He knew what had been done to his body had been the worst profanation. That this body would feed the huge bird that was nourished by the dead seemed to be wholehearted justice.

The path dipped deeper into silence. It was the silence of water dripping within stone, of air's erosion, of light's infinitesimal collapse, it was the silence of existence's slow march toward nothingness, beauty's transformation into an ugliness that was all the more seductive for being irreversible, certainty's descent into shadowier realizations. All that could be done was to follow the path without protesting, even with a sort of joy.

Mary heard the screams not just with her ears but with every part of her body. She had heard the pounding footsteps, the surges of violence that she would never come to understand. Someone had banged on her door. She knew she wouldn't open it. She didn't think to check that the front door had been shut properly, shut and locked and padlocked.

She had gone back into her bedroom, had huddled under her duvet like a wounded animal, like a barely living ghost, and prepared to wait for the furious noise outside, just beneath her window, to stop. (Punches landing, flesh being hammered, bones breaking, she wasn't sure whether she was really hearing it or simply guessing it, or maybe, in her fear, outright imagining it.) It had nothing to do with her. Maybe her neighbors were peeking through their curtains with selfish relief that they were safe in their barricaded houses while the horrific spectacle upended the day's normalcy, but she didn't want to see anything, she would rather have not heard anything, not seen the tortured body with its eyes shut like a reproach for not doing anything. And what could she have done? Called the police? It was far too late for that. By the time they came, there would only be a body, the hooligans would have left, and it would be her door they'd knock at for explanations and eyewitness accounts. It would be no help. And so nobody called the police and all Portobello Road waited, breathless, for the noise to stop and the blows to end and the screams—

The screams. Mary finally heard them. They hadn't been there at first, but now a voice stood out from the other sounds and Mary shivered, Mary got up immediately, Mary jumped out of the bed with a moan, Mary almost yanked apart her curtains to see, at last, to look, to know, and her eyes confirmed what the voice had just told her, that it was indeed Cub, he in a yellow-and-blue cap, he who she had instantly welcomed into her heart, it was he they were beating up, massacring, about to—

She ran every which way in her room. She looked up at the ceiling.

Howard, she yelled, Howard, what should I do?

She went to the phone, the police, maybe it's not too late—

It's no use calling the police, Howard said. You should go and help.

Me? But, Howard . . . They'll make short work of me, that won't help him, I have to think of him and save him, maybe the neighbors . . .

You know your neighbors won't do anything. Look in the mirror, Mary. Don't tell me they won't be terrified of you!

Mary looked at herself in the mirror and saw what Howard saw: a harpy. For once, this ghastly sight suited her. A few seconds later, armed with a kitchen knife, her hair belligerent around her scalp, her jowls drawn tight, looking every bit like an insane skeleton in her fluttering dressing gown, she burst out of the house, shrieking like a siren, frightening the skinheads. They saw her descending upon them and did not realize that she was a very old, barely living woman. Dazed by booze, drugs and blood, they saw a demon come out of the shadows, and they didn't wait one second. Stricken by the same fight-or-flight instinct that had seized Cub earlier, they bolted, leaving behind their victim.

Maybe they would go back to their normal lives, if they'd ever had any. Maybe Mary had stripped them of their taste for violence and blood. There was no way of knowing.

In that moment, Mary fell to her knees in front of Cub's unmoving body.

She did not wait, did not take the time to inspect his wounds or to check whether he was breathing. She leaned down, slipped her arms beneath his body and raised him up with no awareness of just how far such an act was beyond her. He, too, did not know. She carried him into the house, went up the stairs and set him on the bed where the sheets immediately soaked up the blood flowing everywhere.

She refused to believe it could be too late. That there was no point in fighting. That his face was too pale and his lips too white. He was so, so beautiful. It shook her to hold so much beauty in her arms. Such a perfect body entrusted to her hands, offered up to her solitude and her silence. She could have made him, formed him herself, before arthritis had undone her fingers and her dreams had turned toward devastation. She could have shaped the clay to create this outstretched David, this Christlike martyr, this mutilated perfection. She could have hewn his muscles, his neck, his hands. His lips, his cheeks, his eyes, his lashes. His torso, his chest, his stomach, his thighs. His calves, his knees, his feet, his toes. His skull, his hair, his forehead, his nose. The more she looked at him, the more she admired him, no, that verb was weak, she revered him, this pure, animalistic marvel of his body turned so tremulous and so temporary by its very fragility, how could she not adore him, get down on her knees and pay him homage by tracing the lines with her fingers, calling him back to life by infusing him with her own energy, her own blood, her own heartbeat, by instilling him with a regenerative, redemptive love?

In that moment, Mary knew that all her skill in shaping ceramics had been for this one purpose: to refashion Cub, to give him the appearance of life, to offer him eternity. She wrapped him in bandages that, in her eyes, bore no resemblance to shrouds. She tried to warm him again with her own body, the only way of reviving this flesh cooled and discolored too quickly, there had to be this transfer of matter and substance between the two of them, and in this way she knew he was hers, hers alone, and that no one could take him away from her.

She made him a cotton-wool cocoon to keep him warm and did not see the vultures circling in the sky over London. She set him in the nest of his dreams and was not surprised, the next morning, to see his eyes open and watching her solemnly. He was as real as she had wanted him to be.

Sometimes, love can bring about such things.

The days passed and Mary experienced boundless happiness. She had boarded up the doors and closed the shutters. She protected the two of them from all intrusions, including that of the light. No skinhead could threaten Cub anymore. No unknown presence could darken his features.

She cared for him with the same blind patience. She cut up the sheets to make bandages, cleaned his wounds, immobilized his limbs so that his bones would heal. She gave him the medicine that her doctor had prescribed to relieve joint pain for her arthritis, and she was reassured to see him sleeping deeply while his body soldiered on. She washed and scrubbed him carefully, taking great care to move his swollen limbs as little as possible. The dark red wound took the longest to heal. Mary knew it should have been stitched up, but she tightened the cloth bandages as much as she could, and neither her confidence nor her courage let her down.

Little by little, Mary reconstructed the scenario. He hadn't been a wounded animal that had collapsed at her door, but a quiet, small, self-assured man ready to see Mary as something other than an outsider in his life, ready to live and dance with her. They had lived. The two of them had lived together so well.

Outside, winter entered its gloomiest phase. Outside, there was no more sun. The people walking down Portobello Road were bundled-up shadows. They barely bought anything now. The sellers opened up their shops later and later, closed them earlier and earlier. A heavy snow started falling, clinging with stubborn fingers to every surface and refusing to melt. It muffled every noise. Outside, the world entered its emptiest phase. A few lights glowed in the darkness without ever dissipating it. Shapes floated briefly and then disappeared. No sound of cars or trains or planes. Everything had paused, except in the house on Portobello Road, where life wore a mask of joy.

Mary talked to Cub. In his sleepiness he was uncomprehending and unresponsive. But she paid no attention to his silence and sang songs to him, told him stories, made jokes she knew were stupid but which made her laugh like a charming little girl. She dredged up memories she thought she had forgotten, such as the time she learned to make proper British tea, you know, Cub, when I went to Granny's farm, and outside there was sunshine every so often, it wasn't common but it was warm, an early summer sun, and the flowers were still lively. The grass smelled dewy because it was morning, I'd just boiled the water for tea in an old enamel kettle, it had been white at some point but now it was coated in a greasy residue. The kettle was so heavy it took both my hands to pick it up and pour the bubbling water into the teapot I'd warmed up ahead of time, the way Granny taught me. The tea leaves floated up and formed a black, smoky layer on top. When they'd infused enough, they came apart and fell to the bottom of the stout, brown porcelain teapot. Only then was the tea ready to drink, ready to be poured into the teacup where we'd already put a drop of milk that would give it the color of warm gold. That was when I added a spoonful of honey, which would melt so slowly. And at that point I brought the spoon to my mouth to lick the rest of the honey; it tasted like bees.

The sun was as round as a hot loaf of bread just out of Granny's oven. I'll take you there one day, Cub, I'll take you to visit this place, the most beautiful place in the world.

And then, Mary said to Cub, there was Howard, who I met before the war and whose memory has stayed in me like a streak of hot wine. You know he's here, don't you? He's the one living in the attic and watching me through the hole in the ceiling. He's the only man in my life, Cub, the only man I've ever known, the only one I've ever loved, and my entire life on Portobello Road was constructed around this absence, this absent man, until you came. You filled the void.

Howard fought for this country, Cub, for our country, he came back with medals and wounds. That's how things are, Cub, but Howard kept an appetite for life that the others didn't, he was a war veteran, he was a cripple, he was poor and then an outright beggar, but do you know what he really did? He jumped from the top of the Post Office Tower, he fell on a newsstand and he splattered the papers with his blood, Cub, this forgotten beggar hero did that. This is how we live these days, by becoming a paragraph or two in the obits, by taking on significance only when we die, or when we start living without any idea of where we're headed. But Howard overcame all that, he showed me where real life could be found.

We walked through the streets and he showed me something beyond the city's exteriors; he showed me its soft, heavy underbelly, everything that we don't speak or even hear of. I asked him why he killed himself and he told me that he was behind in life. He was quoting a poem to me, but I didn't recognize it. Our life is over, Cub, too much time has gone by since we were young, nothing looks like us now, not Mary the wallflower, not Howard the crippled veteran.

Cub did not reply but Mary was sure she saw him smile. She stroked his forehead. Sleep, Cub, sleep, she said, refusing to acknowledge the twinge in her heart and his increasingly cold extremities. She curled up around him and looked through the window at the strange colors of the sky that did not know her.

And then Mary talked to him about other things, she told him about the towers of silence that Nari, her Parsi neighbor, had described, the black-and-white towers that vultures circled above to clean men's bodies, and the two of them contemplated the beauty of this violence, of this end their imaginations could sense was near, and Mary promised Cub that she would take him to see these towers one day when he was better, I'll use all my savings for that, but so what? I know you want to see them and to discover their secrets.

Howard came down from the attic and set his hand on Mary's shoulder. We'll go, all three of us, Mary, he said. They looked at Cub, sleeping, and tears flowed down their pale cheeks.

And so they stayed, Mary-Howard-Cub, bathed in

their dusty light, half dead, half living, exuding a strange mixture of oldness and youth that seemed like a joyful pollution. They slept. Calmly, gently, softly. She became luminous. Cub, in his sleep, had a childlike innocence, his arms and legs outstretched as if all that space belonged to him. Howard was tanned, dust was embedded in the thousands of wrinkles on his face, the little hair he had left was greasy, his clothes were still those of a beggar, mismatched, shapeless, a mockery of elegance with the worn-out wool jacket, the yellow tie, the moth-eaten vest, the too-large pants held up with a pin, the moccasins. And in him was a wildly energetic laugh that pierced the ever-changing green of his eyes. Glimmers of both irony and tenderness replicated in his mouth with its trembling corners, recreated in his steps as he walked—light, airy, buoyant, as if he could take flight at any moment. He could give a small flick with the tip of his foot, as if he'd just reached the bottom of a body of water, a tiny push to propel himself upward, and he rose up in the air while blowing bubbles, the air carried him upward because he had no substance, and, as in a Chagall painting, the beggar in a flimsy hat and rumpled clothes glided, almost unmoving, in flight over the city, levitating above damp roofs. And, of course, he was dragging behind him his Mary dressed in white and their Cub, their baby wolf. So Mary dreamed in her sleep, refusing to accept that Cub, in front of the door that night, had never woken up.

The house collapsed around them, but they went on living, dancing, laughing, eating. And making love, whether it was two of them, or three, or just one, without any thought to who was who, even if Howard fell apart and Mary's heart threatened to burst. It was a sheer miracle that kept the house on Portobello Road standing. Because they were there, because they refused facts and reality, and because they'd taken the first step into another world free of war, skinheads, aging, youth. They had transformed themselves. Become strange, splendid creatures that no longer touched the ground when they moved.

Cub did not talk anymore. The knife, apparently, had cut his vocal cords. Or, at least, that was what Mary thought, believing as she did whatever she liked. She had cared for him, she had fed him, she had given him life. His eyes were lively enough for her to understand everything he was telling her, for him not to need words, and so words became useless, what use would they be when every particle of air was a vibration? She heard everything and saw everything. Cub's hot-chocolate eyes talked to her of love. They told her that Cub would never leave her again. It was as if she had gathered him into her bosom. She could feel the milk flowing in her breasts, the pain of the newborn child, she who had never been a mother. Stretch marks showed on her rounded belly. Cub wasn't her child, this she knew. What they did have was love.

Mary put on weight. She ate voraciously. She couldn't understand where the provisions in the kitchen cabinets had come from, because she had no memory of going shopping. But there were quality foodstuffs there that she had never bought before, much less tasted: caviar, oysters, quail eggs, lobster. She prepared them expertly, the fish and the meat barely touching the pan because they had such fresh, succulent flavor that they barely needed cooking. The oysters filled her with a taste of the sea so overwhelming that she had the impression of being dipped in sea salt and the ocean breeze. The caviar convinced her a thousand sturgeons had hatched in her stomach. As soon as she peeled a hard-boiled quail egg and placed it in her mouth, she sucked on its smooth surface for a long time without crushing it, her tongue savoring the elastic slickness of the white, her senses refusing to let go of it. Cub shared her meals, complimenting her with his eyes as he relished each plate. In this way she saw him sighing as he tasted a suckling lamb chop from the salt marshes, its meat and fat practically melting as his mouth closed around it. He devoured a dozen, and when he was done, she licked his greasy mouth, the flavor of the cutlets mixed with that of his saliva.

Howard, however, only ate the food after three days. He actually preferred to fish it out of the rubbish after it had started to rot. One day, Mary saw him scarfing down some fish covered in a greenish film. She smiled, not even feeling any disgust. Everything was permitted. She who had tasted dog food could not be shocked by these gamy foods. When she kissed Howard, she inhaled the tainted air of his mouth and she thought to herself that this was the smell of graveyards, of loam, of clay, and that all this was part of the figurines she had started making again. Death, land, life, food, flesh, rot: all that differentiated them was the eye of a woman who had become a perpetual cooking goddess. She formed characters that peopled her house and climbed everywhere like almost-friendly insects on the move. She and Howard played with them, giggling when they tried to hide in terror in the gaps between wooden planks and in the walls. Sometimes she laughed so loudly that she wondered if the neighbors would complain about the noise. But she didn't hear the neighbors now; in fact, she didn't hear any noise at all.

From the other side of the street, Wanda watched the house. Ever since she'd arrived, nobody had come out. She had rung the bell, but nobody had answered. No sign of life. She wondered if someone was still living here, or if Cub had been lying. It had been several days since she'd seen him. For the first time, she was afraid for him. A haze had filled her thoughts ever since that night when she had woken up with Cub's name on her lips and with her heart broken.

Too many traps in this town, in this life. Too many risks and dead ends for her, for Cub, for the girls. The gaps grew as she saw her money disappearing at full speed, nothing in the bank where she no longer dared to go now that her account was overdrawn, her credit cards frozen, notices piling up in her letterbox. All she cared about was bringing something home for her children to eat, not crossing that limit beyond which she would be forced to go to food banks or dig just-expired items from supermarket skips or even ordinary rubbish bins. The sky was threateningly red. The sky over London told her that she had made her choice and now there was no turning back.

Her hours at work had been cut in half. Other women had already been sacked. She was still hanging on, but everyone's gazes were furtive and the implications were clear. The shelves were getting emptier. There were fewer and fewer shoppers, higher and higher discounts, and a sort of desperation had overcome all the employees, as if they knew that, sooner or later, the announcement would be made and their lives would stop. And there was the other letter, the contents of which she already knew but superstitiously refused to open: the date on which the police would come to evict her from the flat she had filled with her dreams and with her own flesh.

Now, as she walked down the street or got on the underground, she noticed the homeless people seemingly multiplying each day. She walked more slowly, looking at them out of the corner of her eye. She saw how they walled themselves off internally so as not to think about how they were living on the sidewalks, visible to all. Their bags, their coats, their boxes, their shopping carts, their scarves, their hats: an accumulation of grayish objects meant to hide them and push away the others; and, indeed, passersby looked away or looked just to the side, rendering them invisible. So they lived outside unseen because nobody wanted to contemplate the obscenity of such a sight. No colors, above all, because colors hinted at a hope they did not have. A sort of burned skin, exposed to the elements here and there like mummies with bandages accidentally torn off. Their eyes were buried beneath hooded eyelashes because they looked at the world from behind a barricade of suspicion. And the world returned the sentiment.

Wanda distanced herself, refusing to imagine that she might end up among these people even as her children were taken away by the state.

Standing in front of Mary's house, she wondered if

she was capable of resisting. How many years had Cub spent looking after himself? How many years ago had she stopped asking him where he was going or even caring? How many years now had Jasmine gone out in her skimpy outfits despite her scolding? She thought about the handbag Cub had brought her, and she smiled. Cub had always been her favorite. Her confidant, her comrade. Ever since his father had left he had been the man of the house. A small werewolf of sorts, as hard as brass, as malleable as iron. Handsome from the day he was born, with his velvety skin and his blossoming lips. His kissable lips, his caressable skin.

Wanda shut her eyes and wanted to slap herself. That's my son, she thought, did I just think about him like . . . like he was a man? A man to love and keep? All the women around her looked at Cub that way. Nobody saw him as a child. Some men were like that, she thought, virile to the core. But I'm his mother.

She looked at Mary's house and asked herself at last: What was Mary doing with Cub? Why had she asked him to live with her? What did she want of him? They hadn't come out for several days. The idea of her magnificent son in the bed of an old hag as pale as a ghost filled her with rage.

She went to knock at the door again when she realized she might need some witnesses if she wanted to get her son back. It wouldn't be hard. In her part of the world, it was easy to rouse up some people. And to convince the authorities that an old white woman was abusing a young black boy—or at least to make sure they didn't take such an accusation lightly. The papers were just waiting for the chance to expose abuse ignored by the authorities. The law was on her side. And all the rights of a mother, a woman, a poor person, a black person.

Wanda raised her fist at the house.

"I'm not letting you steal my son, you shit!" she shouted.

A few passersby glanced at her mistrustfully and steered clear of her path. Others looked away, rendering her invisible.

And so they all came together on Portobello Road, in front of Mary's house.

The members of the gang Cub had belonged to. The Brixton social services. The police constables Wanda had told about Cub's disappearance. The members of Cub's family and their neighbors filled with righteous indignation: no longer simmering in indifference.

Indifference. Everyone around Wanda had been shrouded in indifference for so long. They were all fighting so hard to live that none of them had any time for compassion. But as soon as they had to gather together in indignation and vengeance, they were ready. This made them feel alive. This gave them purpose, an outlet for the impotent rage accumulated in their core. Their homes, their work, their families, their lives had all been stolen. Their gods had been stolen. Brixton had been invaded by property developers who had chopped up their city and who were building invisible walls around them, barriers separating them from the rich, ghettoizing them in the most dangerous neighborhoods. Most of the families were stuck between the gangs and the rich. Today, they would bring down the walls.

In front of Mary's house a group gathered, then a

horde. Most of them had dark skin, but here and there were lighter complexions, the worried faces of officials and the more impassive ones of the police. A social worker knocked at the door. Knocked again for a while. Tried to call Mary's number. She turned to Wanda to ask if she wanted to wait a bit longer, but it was too late.

A boy broke away from the crowd with a bat and shattered the glass pane in Mary's front door. Another threw a rock through the window. A cloud of dust rose up. Wanda let out a scream. They all pressed toward the house.

In the crook of her arm a curly-haired head rested.

No part of him was angular. Nor of her, growing thinner and frailer by the minute, emptying herself the better to welcome him.

Cub slept. His head lay in the junction of Mary's arm, in the groove of the elbow, his cheek rubbing against the softness of the skin there. He was laboriously making his way back from his journey through blood: the world was new. When he awoke again, it seemed reasonable for him to stay beside this woman, to seek the protection of her body, the only one that didn't threaten him like the men who had followed him, who had . . . The nearness had become more terrifying, more somber. Mary watched him dreaming, leaned over him, soaked up his dreams. She leaned a little closer and their lips touched. She would say something every so often, even if he would never understand the sounds of her throat and stomach entering him, bringing him to her, binding him to her.

This boy adrift in her arms, this boy who had lost massive amounts of blood, this boy she had taken in, protected, saved, this boy had become hers as soon as she had given him a second life. His body wasn't cold, it pulsed, oh so gently, so painfully, he shuddered, shook, quaked, he would have gone under but she held him back, held in his blood, pressed her hand flat to hold in everything, so not a drop could escape, and she called him back. Come back, come back. Beads of sweat like shimmering marbles on her brown skin. They seemed to follow one another, then touch one another, bunch together and meld together to form a liquid furrow down her throat, her collar. The faint heartbeat slowed. He relaxed.

This is why I decided not to leave the house anymore, she told him, or you, the cold would break your body, we'll stay here, nice and warm, and we'll have everything we need, you and me both, Cub. After all, it's what this city wanted, everyone's stopped caring about each other, everyone's keeping to themselves, losing themselves in their secret forests, this city only counts its defeated, it tallies them up and strings them on a necklace around its throat, and I want to fight to the bitter end, to be the very last of its trophies, but for how much longer, I don't know.

And this was how they found the two of them as they broke into Mary's bedroom, into a darkness darker than the darkest dark, into the belly of the beast nesting out of everyone's sight, a nest of bloody sheets and dust and shit, reeking of a beast that looked at them with reddened eyes, they would say that afterward, they would testify to the fact that there was no human creature there of flesh and blood, but rather some other thing, they all saw it, and above the bed there was a hole with maggots falling out, and an eye watching them, laughing, and at the center of the nest of sheets and dust and shit was a small, dark, shattered body, naked and swelling, touched by rot already, a small body over which hunched a ferocious, otherworldly creature with fiery eyes.

They would tell their grandchildren about the sight of desolation and danger. It would be a moment of intensity in their lives—as if they didn't have enough already. Many of them, moreover, would not survive the winter. Those who came through it would remember that something had happened that year, a revelation, a shift, a rupture in the world's languid face. The riots, they said, began there: in this scene with a red-eyed creature devouring the boy of legendary beauty.

Wanda understood only one thing in this moment: her child, her little Cub, her little fierce, sleeping animal, was there, below this apparition enveloping him as if he were about to hatch and become something else, deliver out of his body another self, a smoother and handsomer one, but the truth was that her Cub, her baby, wasn't asleep, he was dead, he had long been dead, he had been stolen from her alive and dead by this thing that purported to be a person, that claimed to be a harmless old lady.

Does God in heaven still exist when there are such terrors, such witches come from nowhere, such hellish figures? The old woman looked at Wanda with her red eyes and pointed at her, cackling: "I'm the one who protected him and saved him, I'm the one who loved him and gave birth to him. He belongs to me because you could not bring him back to life!"

Fury rumbled in the people who heard her and who surrounded Wanda. The social worker cut in: "Madam, we're here to take the child. Can you explain how he died? Do you understand what I am saying to you?"

"Who's saying he's dead?" Mary asked. "Jeremiah isn't dead. I saved him from the skinheads attacking him and I took care of him. He's only alive thanks to me and thanks to Howard, the dead beggar in the attic."

Wanda came closer to Cub and saw the gray of his skin, the streaks of his blood, the black of his gangrene, the foul smell rising from the exposed guts in his torso. And she was sure she could see maggots not raining down but in fact breeding within her son's belly.

"She killed my son," Wanda declared.

The men beside her all turned toward Mary. She didn't

see the menace in their eyes. She pushed Wanda back and covered Cub with her body.

"He's alive," she said, "and he's mine."

She did not feel the blows that landed on her body. Afterward, they would make their way to the other houses on Portobello Road, even that of Nari, who wouldn't have a Parsi funeral on a tower of silence, but who would see, in their eyes, the ever-circling vultures.

Mary found herself on the Serpentine's icy curve, on one of these small islands dotting the lake's bend as it angled toward the edge of Hyde Park. The place had a magnificent sadness in winter. A sadness that swept a revived body up in its arms but no longer recognized it. The edges of the sky leaned over her. Its breath, frozen in the cold, ran through her body with a crackling rush. Amid the island's disheveled trees, a few thin storks shivered. The water reflected the sky, which reflected the water. The inverted island seemed far more real. The island was like the country. Always far more real in her own dreams.

Mary sat at the water's edge. She was wearing a white cotton dress, crumpled and creased from sitting down. Her legs were bare and far too white. Her feet, too, were bare. She wasn't cold. She inhaled, her eyes closed.

The scent of old algae, she thought to herself. Of a lost lagoon. Places like this spoke to her of legends. Do you hear the castles sinking beneath the water?

Everything seemed older, the lichen licking the stones there where the waves splashed as they broke, the marks of old tides, the hoary trees contorted painfully by the winds, the mournful gaze of the low hills covered in rubbish. She entered the space as if into open arms, she only had to inhale to take in the history, the stories, the memories, the moments, the countless pasts, the tales, the legends that men had tried to relegate to uselessness, without ever quite succeeding, because their animalistic sighs kept on warming her neck.

Mary plunged her feet into the water and breathed in. She leaned back to look at the underside of the weeping willow overhanging her. Apple-green, chicken-green, heart-green, she thought, and then stem-green. She giggled.

Cub had joined her. She stood up. Her feet crushed the few blades of close-cut grass, her body unfurled as she raised her arms up. Her oddly angled shoulder blades were ready to spread out, to stretch out. What was next? Would she take flight, leaving Cub behind? He could have slept and died in his neighborhood, in front of his mother, in solitude or in violence. The cold had already seeped into his bones. He could have died down there, and slept.

For the moment he was there, beside her, watching her extend her wings.

Taste the air, she said. She seemed to hear its invisible jingling in her hand. Like salt dissolving with a sizzling whisper.

You've taken a step out of this world.

They stayed the whole day on the island. At sunset, they saw the shadows of boats carrying the shadows of rowers gliding silently over the water. This was not the indolent happiness of hot summer nights. This was a dazed, disjointed pavane in which the Sunday rowers and boatmen pressed toward nowhere.

For Cub, this was like a small triumph: he had never believed in these families, in their games. When he was a teenager, a thread had snapped. The children so adored when they were born were no longer beloved. Each one hid behind resentment: the sneering parents and the broken children. In the parks, children over ten were never with their parents. When they were older they were sentenced to prowling on the edges of decomposed family units.

The small boats went by, one after another. The families, the couples, the teenagers discovered new relationships that were just as ephemeral, that would break apart the families already headed toward rupture. In winter's gloomy reflections, generations disappeared behind other generations. This time, the Serpentine wouldn't circle back on itself. Once they had passed the enclosed space that preserved memories of laughter, the boats dissolved with their cargo, never to return. This unusual sadness gave Cub the feeling that he wouldn't have any more summers. A permanent winter was now swallowing him up. It was the final season of the park, of the city, of this island within an island. It was the final season of all.

Cub began to cry, because he had come to understand that, despite his jealousy, or perhaps because of it, he clung to these families as if to a secret hope and wanted to give them a sad farewell.

Seven heavens claim the sky. Emptiness has levels. Likewise
solitude, which is the emptiest of heaven and earth, the emptiness
of man, in whom it stirs and breathes.

—EDMOND JABÈS, *Of Solitude as the Space of Writing*,
translated by Rosmarie Waldrop

And now that he knew, he could see his own slowly decomposing body in Mary's bedroom, liquefied by the dampness of this airless space. He saw what he had become. He saw the primal, primary ugliness of his flesh now that the fiber of life had abandoned him. That's what we've been carrying within ourselves all this time, he thought. We who had been so alive had been headed this way. This perfect disintegration that leaves no room for dignity, for beauty. A shapeless, sticky, sickening mass. He looked at himself and he was no longer sure whether he was here or there, the putrefying body or the wandering spirit now detached from everything; maybe he was just a fillip of energy floating up from this body that, orphaned, would soon dissipate in the air with nothing to make it stay, or even return. Return to what, anyway? There was nothing here to tempt him now.

He sees the heavier cold coming from the east, about to catch them in its grip. Immense clouds laden with snow and ice are approaching. The lilac sky readies itself, closes up, becomes mirrorlike. Nobody can see it yet, but all this has been forecast. The clouds will stop here, right here, over the silent, sleeping city, and soon they will unleash their storm. They will catch the people sure of clement weather by surprise. Everything will come undone. As usual, some will say. But this will not be as usual. This polar chill will not be like any other. It will be borne by the cold in so many hearts, by the children killed on a street corner or on a set of stairs, by women trapped within their walls of incomprehension, by a lack of freedom—oh, that word, that warm always-denied word—and the chill that will come from deep below to join the one descending from above will freeze the weather, ice and snow will fix everything where it is, a permanent and perennial immobility that will be beautiful, too. A white-and-blue hand will close on London and, slowly, crush it.

In the distance, he senses, although he cannot see, the massive bulks of King's Cross St Pancras. He hears the groans of stone and alabaster and human dust. He sees their immense black spaces, the shadows that flash beneath the crossbeams, beneath the vaults. He senses that the beginning and the end will be there. And now the roofs of the two interlocked train stations open partway. The cold arrives, an impossibly large, noisome slap. The wind heralds it. The clouds swirl in a rush as in a horror film. They are black, and the day is shuttered. Lower down, on the street, people look up and stare dumbly at the arctic winter descending upon them. They raise their arms to protect themselves, then they run in search of shelter. The dampness becomes iciness, forming a slippery film over the surfaces. The hurried footsteps slip and stumble. The houses are shaken as if by a seismic sigh. Joints crack.

Above the train station, winged forms take to the air. Cub watches them; he is unquestionably the only one to see them. He knows that these are the creatures that attacked him, skinheads that could sometimes take on a semihuman form but which were in fact creatures from beyond the grave, come to dig their hateful claws into human flesh, come to inject their hateful venom into human souls. They take on gargoyles' masks, they shriek as they scatter across the city, their droppings are gigantic hailstones, they assault and stun and end up sucking dry all the life, all the warmth that remains in petrified bodies. To believe that these are the screams of the wind would be no more reassuring.

The streets are covered, one by one, in the white dust. On Oxford Street, the huge stores are blinded, their glass fronts latticed by the brutal frost. The holiday lights burst one by one. The red buses skid and come to a halt as they block the roads. The sharp, gilded, red notes that Cub had heard shatter.

A beggar is found dead from the cold, his lips stuck to his flute from which wan melodies still escape. The people flee this desolate sight, but no part of town is spared. In Regent's Park, immense curtains of ice hang from the trees, forming a labyrinth that nobody dares to enter. Within, sounds are frozen in place by the crystal, then refracted into infinity. The small lakes disappear within the surrounding white. The Thames begins to flow more and more slowly, with more and more difficulty, until millions of small branches knit together beneath its surface and stop its progress. Some storks land there, astounded as they walk on the waves. They seem to be trampling inverted humans underfoot. On the banks, a couple in love die in their ecstasy, their half-naked bodies turning blue at the peak of orgasm. It will be impossible to separate them. They will be buried together with what will have been captured for the first time on their unmoving faces as the purest expression of the magnificent pain of love.

The trains, too, stop. Antennae snap. No more communication. No more mobile phones. No more internet. No more signals of any kind circulating, racing, slipping from one to another, connecting people less and less than they think, orphaning them even to themselves. The precious abstraction of our modern life—energy in all its forms—buckles beneath the assault of this other primal, primary energy that is nature. Man, in his protective bubble, realizes that he has no way of defending himself and that nature has always been playing cat and mouse with him. In no time at all, with a casual flick, it can sweep away everything he has built and destroy it as swiftly as an animal's curt shriek.

And Mary, too, of course . . . She who had always been so scared, so scared of the cold . . . she will be pierced, stabbed, impaled by it. Nothing will have prepared her for this, not even her deep-rooted dread of winter, especially the ferrous winter which was the most deceptive and the most implacable sort, not even the numbness as she waits at first, as her body prepares to shrivel up and crackle in extreme temperatures. No, this time, it bears no resemblance to what she had known. It is an archaic cold, come from ice ages long since forgotten but which have awaited an opportune moment to resurge. A cold that crushes the very memory of heat. That seizes blood in the very motion of its flowing and arrests it with a mortal jolt. That makes bodies strange to themselves even as they escape to this other reality where immobility is the only possible or even desirable state.

She becomes like the city: still, feeble, fragile. Barely convinced that she is still alive, she lies down; she lets herself be taken and invaded; she is ready to give herself over to this state that suddenly seems to be a gentle, almost euphoric, way to die. "Hypothermia," she whispers as an incantation, feeling the corners of her mouth freeze. Her lips are no longer able to part. Her eyelashes stick to her eyelids. The usual pains give way to another sensation that she, in her sleepiness, cannot quite identify. Her legs have separated. She begins to turn blue.

After some time, she feels Cub's presence. She tries to see him through the eyelashes that have crosshatched her vision.

"Are you there?" she asks. "Is that you, Cub?"

"It's me and it isn't," he replies. "I don't know what miracle made it possible for you to hide the truth of my own death. We all believed that illusion. People saw me, I'm sure of it. But you didn't just see me, you touched me, caressed me, took me in your arms. You let me go on believing that I was alive, just a little, for a few more nights. I still remember that dizziness . . . You were a benevolent spirit who embraced me at the moment I was the most bereft, the most desolate. You forgot yourself for my sake. You walked into guilt and you did not waver."

Cub kneels in front of her and sets his hand on the icy body. He has no substance, no materiality. What he gives is warmth as he brings her limbs back to life, sets her blood flowing again with a pleasant pain through her blue fingernails and fingers, her bruised phalanges, her thighs crisscrossed with veins like cracks in an antique porcelain vase, her weak, slow, sad shoulders, her neck rigid with shame, her lips which had silently rejected what was beneath the surface, a sensual burn, an inexhaustible thirst within her body for bodies, for flesh, for nearness, for invasion. He plunges into Mary to return what she had given him, and their joy is brief but complete.

Finally she stretches her limbs and stands up again.

She has only just understood what he told her earlier. She tries to remember that night, but she cannot. She has a vague impression of a body up in the attic, but no, it was here, this body, with her, it was there, in her, there is no possibility she could be wrong about this.

"You have to go, now," he says.

"Go where? I'd rather die here. I don't have the choice. I was never alive. If you're dead, then I've been dead, too, and for far longer."

He feels, unfurling deep within him, a thousand icy blossoms.

ANANDA DEVI was born in Mauritius in 1957, and currently lives in France. She has published thirteen novels as well as short stories and poetry, and has won several literary awards, including the Académie française's Prix du Rayonnement de la langue et de la littérature françaises.

JEFFREY ZUCKERMAN is the digital editor for literature of *Music & Literature* magazine. He previously translated Ananda Devi's *Eve Out of Her Ruins* and his other translations include Jean Genet's *The Criminal Child*.

More Translated Literature
from the Feminist Press

Arid Dreams: Stories by Duanwad Pimwana,
translated by Mui Poopoksakul

August by Romina Paula,
translated by Jennifer Croft

La Bastarda by Trifonia Melibea Obono,
translated by Lawrence Schimel

Beijing Comrades by Bei Tong,
translated by Scott E. Myers

Chasing the King of Hearts by Hanna Krall,
translated by Philip Boehm

The Iliac Crest by Cristina Rivera Garza,
translated by Sarah Booker

Mars: Stories by Asja Bakić
translated by Jennifer Zoble

The Naked Woman by Armonía Somers,
translated by Kit Maude

Pretty Things by Virginie Despentes,
translated by Emma Ramadan

The Restless by Gerty Dambury,
translated by Judith G. Miller

**Testo Junkie: Sex, Drugs, and Biopolitics
in the Pharmacopornographic Era** by Paul B. Preciado,
translated by Bruce Benderson

Women Without Men by Shahrnush Parsipur,
translated by Faridoun Farrokh